She was looking at a pirate!

Meredith ran her finger over the illustration in the old book, *Rogues Across Time,* taking in each detail. Ever since she was a little girl, she'd always been fascinated by the legends surrounding those fearless sea rovers. But as she grew older, the fascination had fueled a bizarre fantasy. In her dreams, the pirate, a devilishly handsome rogue, would come to her at midnight. His hand would cover her mouth as she put up a half-hearted struggle. And then he'd carry her off to his ship....

A loud crash of thunder startled her, drawing her attention away from the book. She held up the lantern and stared out at the darkness. A flash of white caught her eye and Meredith squinted to see what it was. Slowly, she walked toward the beach, keeping her eyes on the strange shape. Only when she stood directly over the form did she realize she was looking at a man. A very familiar man....

"Oh, Lord," she murmured.

Dear Reader,

One of the best things about romance novels is that I get to fall in love right along with my heroine. And never has that been more true than with the hero of *The Pirate,* my ninth book for Temptation. From the moment Griffin Rourke appeared in my mind and on the pages of my manuscript, I knew he'd be a special hero—a man impossible to resist. After all, he brought with him all the chivalry and valor of an age long past. And he was pretty darn handsome, too!

As I lay in bed last winter with my leg in a cast (the result of a nasty fall on the ice), I began to spin the story of how Griffin came to be in our time. And as I wrote, Griffin began to spin his own kind of magic, pulling both me and my heroine, Meredith Abbott, under his spell. When I finally sent the manuscript off to my editor, I wondered whether Griffin would have the same effect on her as he did on me. I didn't have to wait long for her answer. She soon called with the news that she, too, had lost her heart to Griffin.

Now it's time to share this hero with all of you, my readers. I hope you enjoy *The Pirate.* And I also hope that you lose a little piece of your heart to Griffin Rourke!

Happy Reading,

Kate Hoffmann

P.S. I love to hear from my readers. Please write to me c/o Harlequin Temptation, 225 Duncan Mill Road, Don Mills, Ontario, Canada M3B 3K9

THE PIRATE
Kate Hoffmann

Harlequin Books

TORONTO • NEW YORK • LONDON
AMSTERDAM • PARIS • SYDNEY • HAMBURG
STOCKHOLM • ATHENS • TOKYO • MILAN
MADRID • WARSAW • BUDAPEST • AUCKLAND

For my friend, fellow writer, proficient plotter, and trusty
traveling companion, Pamela Johnson, who made a five-day
round-trip from Wisconsin to Ocracoke Island much more
fun than a research trip should ever be.

And with special thanks to Mickey Roberson,
Blackbeard expert and owner of "Teach's Hole,"
Ocracoke, North Carolina, for all her help in bringing
Blackbeard and Ocracoke to life for me.

ISBN 0-373-25677-9

THE PIRATE

Copyright © 1996 by Peggy Hoffmann

Printed in U.S.A.

ROGUES

ROGUES ACROSS TIME

THE PIRATE

'Twas the golden age of piracy, a time when rogues of the sea plied the waters of the world, marauding and pillaging, their very existence becoming a plague on all maritime activities. Though a pirate's life was more likely to end on the gallows than in idle retirement, by the 1700s both men and women had taken up the profitable trade.

Gentleman Harry and Calico Jack, Anne Bonny and Mary Read—these pirates were among the elite members of the "Brethren of the Coast." But the most fearsome of all these rovers was the notorious Blackbeard. Bold and daring, frightening in appearance and utterly fearless, Blackbeard's meteoric rise to power struck terror into the hearts of all seagoing men sailing the coastal waters of the American colonies.

More than one man had wished for the end to Blackbeard's days on earth. But only one man had made a solemn vow to see it done. That man was Griffin Rourke.

1

A LONG SHRIEK sliced through the night like a banshee's lament, rattling the windows and whirling around the cottage until the wail obliterated everything but the pounding of her heart in her throat and the taste of panic in her mouth. Meredith Abbott wedged herself farther into the corner of the musty closet and buried her face in her knees, pressing her bent arms against her ears.

"It'll be over soon," she murmured to herself. "It can't go on forever. It can't."

This very same terror had haunted her childhood, but after so many years of undisturbed sleep, Meredith had assumed she'd outgrown the nightmare. After all, she was a woman now, nearly twenty-nine years old—a woman reliving the most frightening night of her life.

While other children may have dreamed of dragons beneath the bed or cackling crones lurking in the shadows, Meredith had dreamed of Hurricane Delia. And now, with another Delia screaming outside the windows of the gray-shingled cottage, Meredith's fears had returned with such astounding clarity that she wondered if she had ever really left them behind.

"Shiver me timbers! *Awwwk!* Thar she blows!"

"Shut up, Ben!" Meredith whispered. The gray parrot flapped its wings, the movement eerily illuminated on the closet walls like some bizarre shadow-puppet game. The electricity had failed six hours ago and all she had to scare away the dark and her demons was an old hurricane lamp, the flame sputtering and swaying with every draft that slipped beneath the closet door.

"Would you perchance have a piece of cheese?" Ben inquired, punctuating the request with a wolf whistle and another squawk.

If she hadn't been so preoccupied with her phobias, Meredith probably would have throttled the bird then and there. First, he'd presented a recitation of every nautical cliché in the book and now, he'd started quoting his namesake, Ben Gunn from *Treasure Island.* But in all honesty, she was glad she didn't have to face Delia alone. She'd faced the hurricane alone when she was just a child and the experience had haunted her until the day she'd sailed away from Ocracoke Island on the Hatteras ferry.

"Yo ho ho, and a bottle of rum!" Ben cried.

"Rum," Meredith repeated. "I could use a good stiff drink right now. Are you buying?"

"I takes my man Friday with me!"

"Ah, *Robinson Crusoe* now, is it? Imagine my luck. I'm sharing a closet with a parrot more widely read than most of my graduate students."

"Aye, matey."

Maybe she shouldn't have come back to Ocracoke after all, but it had seemed the perfect setting to work on her newest scholarly endeavor. She'd taken a year's sabbatical from her teaching position at the College of William and Mary to finish her biography on Blackbeard—the book that would assure her spot on the top of the list for the Sullivan Fellowship. And once she'd been awarded the fellowship, she'd be first in line for a tenured position. After that, she planned to be the youngest department chairperson on campus.

She had arrived on the island off the coast of North Carolina right after Labor Day, and for reasonable rent, she'd set up housekeeping in a roomy cottage on the water overlooking Pamlico Sound and Teach's Hole, the channel where the infamous Blackbeard had once anchored his sloop, *Adventure*.

The first three weeks had been idyllic, the simple rhythms of island life settling back into her blood. Once an Ocracoker, always an Ocracoker, they'd told her. She'd been accepted into the tight-knit community as if she'd never left. After all, her father had been an islander and these people had all but raised her after her mother died. She was family and she'd come home.

When the first storm warnings had sounded, she'd considered leaving the island on the next ferry, but instead, she'd stupidly decided to face her fears and ride out the storm. After all, Horace had been declared only a tropical storm, not yet a dreaded hurricane like Delia, and Ocracoke had weathered much worse.

By the time Horace had been upgraded to a category-one hurricane, it had been too late to leave. The ferries were safely moored on the mainland and she was left to face eighty-mile-per-hour winds, driving rain and a surging sea—alone.

Meredith leaned back against the wall. It was nearly midnight and the wind still howled outside, the rain scratching against the glass like a hag's fingernails. She didn't have the courage to venture out of the safety of the bedroom closet—not until the storm showed signs of weakening. She grabbed the lantern and held it up to survey her cramped surroundings, desperate for anything to occupy her mind. A stack of books at her elbow caught her eye and she pulled a dusty volume off the top.

The smell of mildew touched her nose as she held the book up to the lantern light. The gold inlaid letters on the cover were burnished by age, but the title was still legible.

Rogues Across Time. The author's name was worn from the spine, and a dark stain obliterated the name on the title page.

She turned back the leather-bound cover and the book fell open to an illustration, a finely rendered, black-and-white drawing—of a pirate. A shiver ran through her at the strange coincidence, another in a long line of happenstance, little bits of luck and good fortune that seemed to be tossed in her path by some greater force.

"Stop scaring yourself," she said out loud. "Everything happens for a logical reason. You don't believe in fate."

Still, she could understand why a person might. When she'd arrived at the real-estate office after disembarking the ferry, she'd been told that the old cottage she'd originally rented on the wooded path called Howard Street was not available. Instead, the real-estate agent had given her the keys to a larger cottage on the water—overlooking the exact spot where Blackbeard used to drop anchor. Twist of fate number one.

The cottage came along with twist of fate number two, the owner's pet parrot, a salty-tongued bird that would have made any sailor a fine companion. With Ben Gunn sitting on his perch spouting "nauticisms" and Meredith at her computer, the atmosphere had seemed perfect for writing the definitive biography of Blackbeard. She had never worked harder or written better in her life.

And then came Horace—twist of fate number three. A hurricane hadn't hit the island for more than twelve years. But then again, hurricanes usually hit the Outer Banks in nine-year cycles, so she really couldn't count Horace as fate, and he certainly couldn't be considered good fortune.

Now, as she stared down at the picture of the pirate, an overwhelming sense of apprehension assailed her, as if she was suddenly powerless against this greater force. Something was about to happen, she could feel it in the air, and it frightened her.

"Stop it!" Meredith scolded.

"Stop it!" Ben mimicked.

"This storm's got me so tense I'm beginning to imagine things."

She purposefully returned her attention to the book, running her finger over the illustration, taking in each detail. The pirate had long dark hair that framed aristocratic features. He wore knee breeches, a flowing white linen shirt and a dark waistcoat. Two leather straps crisscrossed his chest with small pistols tucked in loops along them. In his right hand was a short, curved cutlass, and tucked into his belt, a dagger.

Meredith was surprised by the accuracy of the drawing, considering Hollywood's imprint on the image of a pirate—eye patch and peg leg, tricorn and gold earring, and the requisite bird on the shoulder. Her gaze drifted back to his face. All right, so maybe the drawing wasn't entirely accurate. This pirate looked more like one of those male models that appeared in designer-underwear ads than a real buccaneer from the bounding main.

She focused on the illustration, trying to block out the weather that raged around the cottage, allowing the image to drift off the page and into her mind. Since her girlhood, she'd been fascinated by the legends of pirates, the ruthless men who plied the waters of the Outer Banks, preying on ships with merciless abandon. It was with the stories of pirates that her love of history took root.

But as she'd grown older, the fascination had fueled a bizarre fantasy, a fantasy so uncharacteristic of her normal, conservative nature that she'd been embarrassed to even think about it. The notion was borne of pure romance and based on nothing resembling reality.

In her dreams, the pirate, a devilishly handsome rogue, would come to her at midnight, slipping into her bedroom. His hand would cover her mouth as she put up a halfhearted struggle. After he'd bound her hands and gagged her, he would toss her over his shoulder and take her to his ship. From there, the fantasy would become more erotic, a sensual dance between a predator and his prey.

But that was as far as the fantasy ever went. She'd usually wake up before the first item of clothing was discarded and no matter how hard she tried to resume the dream, she'd never managed to complete it.

Why bother? She knew how it would end. Her fear of intimacy would overwhelm her and she'd run away...the same way she had in real life. At first, she'd blamed her fears on practicality. Outside of her work, she had little room in her life for a real relationship. But as time passed, she realized that all the years spent in scholastic pursuits, her nose buried in history books while other girls thought only about boys, had done little to prepare her for a real relationship. She had less knowledge of the opposite sex than the average nun.

"I was born too late," Meredith murmured as she stared at the drawing. She'd always wanted to live in an earlier time, when life was more immediate, more exciting—when men were heroic and courageous and chivalrous. And women were modest . . . and virginal.

But since that hadn't been possible, she'd chosen the next best thing—she had majored in history in college and spent her life reading and writing about the past. Her doctoral dissertation focused on American maritime history—to be specific, colonial pirates and privateers.

"Call me Ishmael," Ben implored in a raucous voice.

Meredith jumped at the sound, clutching the open book to her breast. "I'll call you parrot potpie if you don't stop with the quotes!" she replied. The image of the bird between two pastry crusts brought a hesitant smile. "Parrot potpie," she repeated. "Yum, yum."

"*Awk!* Parrot potpie," Ben mimicked. "Yum, yum."

Meredith glanced back down at the pirate and traced her finger along the lines of his face. Strange how he looked so much like the man in her dreams. As she held the book, she felt a pulsing warmth seep into her icy hands. Suddenly, the book seemed to vibrate with a life of its own. Startled, Meredith drew in a sharp breath and quickly snapped it shut before replacing it on top of the stack.

She wasn't sure how long she stared at the closed volume, trying to arouse the fantasy again, but when Ben ruffled his wings, attracting her attention, she dragged her gaze away. Only then did she realize that an eerie silence had descended on the cottage. The wind had stilled and the rain now drummed softly on the roof. She glanced down at her watch. It read exactly midnight.

She drew a deep breath and pushed open the closet door, then unfolded her stiff legs and crawled out. Ben flapped out behind her. The lantern illuminated the bedroom around her, casting giant shadows on the walls.

She made a quick survey of the house's interior, finding very little damage—just a few broken windowpanes in the bathroom. After placing the parrot back on his perch, she continued her search for destruction.

The screened porch which overlooked the Sound hadn't fared well. She stepped out the door, picking her way through twisted wire mesh, upended lawn furniture and debris from the live oaks scattered about the property. Warily, Meredith made her way down the stairs and out to the yard. The calm was unnerving after the chaos just a few minutes before.

The waves still crashed against the shore, encroaching on the lawn with every surge. But the rain, no longer blown into stinging shards, now seemed almost as soothing as a springtime shower.

She held up the lantern and stared out into the darkness. A flash of white caught her eye and Meredith squinted to see what it was. An odd piece of flotsam, half-black, half-white, lay on the lawn, just beyond the reach of the water. Slowly, she walked across the surf-saturated grass, keeping her eyes on the strange shape. It moved once, but she was certain it had only been a play of light or the breeze, even though the air was deadly calm.

Common sense told her to return to the house and assess the damage in the light of day, but she found herself drawn to the water's edge. Only when she stood directly over the form did she realize she was looking at a man.

"Oh, Lord!" she murmured. Dropping onto one knee, Meredith placed the lantern near his head and gently turned him from his side to his back. He moaned softly but didn't regain consciousness. His long wet hair was plastered across his face and she pushed it away. A thick black beard obscured his features, but there was something about him that seemed familiar. So familiar, and yet entirely nameless. Even in the dim light, she was certain she didn't know this man.

He was wearing a torn white shirt, an odd vest, and, of all things, breeches. A pair of black leather boots covered his feet and legs to the knee. And around his waist was fixed a scabbard which held no weapon.

Meredith groaned. "I should have known. You're one of Tank Muldoon's boys."

Trevor Muldoon, known on the island as "Tank," ran a waterfront tourist trap, a restaurant and bar called the Pirate's Cove. All of his waiters dressed as pirates, adding to the restaurant's ambience and popularity. But most of the waiters were rowdy college kids who'd left the island right after Labor Day.

"What did you do?" Meredith scolded. "Slam down a few rum punches before you decided to experience a hurricane firsthand?" She shook his shoulder. "Come on, get up before the tide washes you away."

He moaned again and turned his head toward her. A trickle of blood slid down along his temple before the rain washed it away. Meredith cursed softly. She couldn't just leave him out here, but what else was she supposed to do? He was too big to pick up and carry into the house.

She drew a deep breath and tried to calm her jangled nerves. She should phone for help. The police would come and drag him away to jail, giving him time to dry out before they sent him on his merry way.

An errant breeze played at the flame of the lantern. She sucked in a sharp breath as a wash of light fell across the man's face. Even though his shaggy hair and beard made him appear uncommonly fierce, right now he looked vulnerable, helpless.

Slowly, she reached out and brushed the rain off his forehead, her fingers tracing his strong features. As she felt his damp skin beneath her fingers, her breath stopped in her throat. He was so cold, so still. A shiver skittered down her spine and she snatched her hand away and clutched it to her chest.

Warily, she stood, then backed away from him, filled with a strange sense of foreboding. He was a perfect stranger and she should be frightened. Meredith Abbott was usually leery of pretty much everything, especially men. But this man, lying half-dead on her beach, didn't scare her.

No, what truly frightened her were the forces that had brought him here.

MEREDITH FLOPPED DOWN onto the floor, every muscle in her body aching with cold and exhaustion. Her pirate lay sprawled next to her on the couch where she'd finally settled him after dragging him inside. Ben stared at them both from his perch in the corner, silent, suspicious of the stranger.

As soon as she'd closed the door behind him, the wind and rain had kicked up again, almost on cue, resuming its former fury. But this time, she couldn't run for the closet. The pirate didn't look at all well and, at the moment, she was the only one available to tend to him. She efficiently gathered all the candles and lanterns from the rest of the house and brought them into the living room. The cottage was well-stocked with both, for the island suffered power outages during most storms.

As she set a kerosene lamp on the coffee table, the pirate moaned again, then muttered something she couldn't understand. His expression suddenly turned angry, agitated, and she was again reminded of how menacing the man looked. His clothes were in tatters and his face was covered with a scruffy black beard. Tall and broad-shouldered, he barely fit on the couch. She gently pushed his shoulders back and in a few moments he relaxed. If he were lucid, she knew she'd be no match for his strength.

With a shaking hand, she reached over and placed her palm on his cheek. His skin was still cold and the rise and fall of his chest nearly imperceptible. The scrape on his forehead had stopped bleeding, but he had other wounds more serious than a simple abrasion. A quick examination revealed a knot the size of a golf ball on the back of his head, several cuts and scrapes on his jaw beneath his beard and a nasty bruise on his left knee.

"Couldn't you just have gotten drunk and passed out on your own couch?" she said in a small voice. "I don't know what to do. I'm not a doctor. And I have no way to get help, not until the storm breaks."

She'd tried to call the police, but the phones were out. The sheriff's deputy and his assistant, who served as the island's police force, were probably well occupied with other problems. She would have tried the neighbors, but she already knew the houses on either side of her cottage belonged to summer residents. And the island's doctor visited the small medical clinic only once a week. For the present, she was this man's sole help.

If she were brave, she'd venture out and find help. But the opening in the storm that had allowed her to rescue him had quickly closed. She'd have to walk at least a quarter mile to the main road and hope to flag down the sheriff. Meredith sat up on her heels and rubbed her eyes. Suddenly, the weather outside seemed insignificant compared to what was happening inside the cottage.

"Where did you come from? And why did you have to pick my beach?"

She idly brushed his tangled hair back from his face. His eyelids fluttered and then opened. He stared up at her, his pale blue eyes empty, uncomprehending, as if he were looking right through her.

She leaned forward. "Can you hear me?" Meredith asked. "Who are you? What happened?"

He opened his mouth and tried to speak, but all he could manage was a raspy croak. As if the effort was too much, his eyes closed again and his harsh breathing settled back into a shallow, even rhythm.

"I don't even know what to call you," she murmured. "You must have a name." Meredith crawled to the end of the couch and tugged at his knee-high boots. "Maybe I'll call you Ned. Ned, the pirate. You know, Blackbeard's nickname was Ned, for Edward." She glanced over at him and shook her head. "I guess you're not in any condition to complain about my choice, are you Ned?"

After a long struggle, the wet boot suddenly slipped free of his foot. Meredith landed on her backside, the boot in her lap. She stared down at it, stiff leather around the calf and a flared top that formed a cup around the knee. She turned the boot over in her hand and looked at the sole.

"This is a handmade boot," she murmured. Meredith tugged the other boot off and examined it closely, searching for a brand name or a label. "Jackboots. These boots haven't been made since the early eighteenth century. Where did you ever find a cobbler to . . ."

Her voice trailed off as her eyes moved up from his rough woolen stockings to his breeches. Like the boots, they were handmade, fitted at the leg and baggy at the waist. Glancing nervously at his face, she plucked at the fly with her fingers, causing a flood of heat to rush to her cheeks. "Hmm, no zipper, just buttons. Very authentic." Her confusion was deepened even further by his tattered linen shirt, full at the sleeves and ruffled at the wrist. There was no tag in the neckline, only very fine hand stitching on the band collar.

The shirt lay open nearly to his waist. She stared down at his deeply tanned chest, mesmerized by the play of candlelight on the rippled muscle. With a small pang of uneasiness, she pushed the damp linen together, her hand brushing against the light dusting of hair that ran from his collarbone to his belly.

All of his clothes were wet, but Meredith wasn't about to remove them. Not that she wasn't curious as to what he looked like beneath the odd garments. It wasn't every day she had a man lying helpless on her couch. But there were limits to her nursing skills and to her temerity.

Instead, she pulled a throw from the back of the rocking chair and tucked it around his body. Then she dragged a quilt from the guest bedroom and arranged that on top of him. By the time she'd finished building a fire, his breathing seemed less labored and the color had begun to return to his lips.

She drew a steadying breath. "All right, Ned, now that you're warm, we'd better take care of your wounds. After that, I'll make some coffee and we'll sober you up."

A quick search of the medicine cabinet in the bathroom turned up alcohol, bandages, shaving cream, a straight-edged razor and a small pair of scissors. After bandaging the scrape on his forehead, Meredith tucked a towel around Ned's neck and began to snip away at his salt encrusted beard. She staunched the bleeding from the cuts with the towel before she gently covered his face with shaving cream.

With great care for his wounds, she drew the razor along his cheek. Stroke by stroke, she carefully stripped away the remains of his dirty beard, intent on her task. When she was finished, Meredith drew back. She blinked in shock, clutching the razor in her fist as her gaze fell on the planes and angles of a startlingly handsome face. Until this instant, she'd had nothing more than a nagging fear of this stranger, of having this man alone in her house with help so far away.

As she stared down at his perfect features, Meredith found herself hypnotized. She *had* seen him before, just hours ago as she focused on the illustration of the pirate in the old book. Pinching her eyes shut, she tried to steady her spinning thoughts. If she had believed in the powers of fate, she might have also believed that she'd somehow summoned him here to answer her girlish fantasies.

But she knew better. He was merely one of Tank Muldoon's boys, she repeated to herself, out to tear up the town right alongside Hurricane Horace. And yet, even though that explanation seemed perfectly logical, it didn't make sense. This was a grown man, not a college boy. No one developed a body like his waiting tables—he worked hard for a living, probably outdoors. And no one took Tank Muldoon seriously enough to wear an authentic costume.

Meredith leaned over to wipe a trace of shaving cream from his cheek. Suddenly, his hand snaked up and clamped onto her wrist in a punishing grip. She cried out and tried to pull away, but he held her fast. Her gaze met his. His pale blue eyes were now lucid and hard as ice. They watched each other for a very long time in the dim light, Meredith's pulse thudding in her throat, his breathing harsh and even.

"Where am I?" he demanded, his voice ragged.

Meredith tried to pull out of his grasp again, but he only tightened his fingers.

"Tell me, lad. Who are you?"

"Lad?" Meredith asked.

He easily twisted her wrist and brought the razor she was holding flat against her throat. "Who brought me to this place?" he asked, enunciating each word, a slight brogue to his proper British accent. "Have a care, for I will know if you speak falsely."

"I—I brought you here," Meredith whispered. "You were washed up on the beach during the storm."

"The purse, where is it?"

"You want my purse?"

"The purse," he said, his grip weakening. "I . . . I must deliver . . . proof . . . upon my soul . . . I must . . . avenge . . . father . . ." His eyes rolled back in his head and his hand flopped down on his chest, suddenly lifeless, boneless.

"Have a care!" Ben squawked from the shadows.

Meredith quickly retreated from the couch, watching the man from a spot near the fireplace. If she wasn't frightened of Ned before, she certainly was now. He was a madman, muttering about purses and revenge in some hokey British accent. She could still feel the cold blade of the razor against her throat. Her fingers flexed and the straight-edge clattered to the wooden floor. Without thinking, she wrapped her grip around the fireplace poker instead.

She turned and raced to the closet for her slicker. She couldn't stay here. She'd have to summon the sheriff before her pirate woke again. But when she pulled open the front door, the reality of the situation slapped her in the face.

The wind ripped the door from her hand, slamming it back against the wall with stunning force. Debris whipped through the air and the rain stung her skin like a hail of tiny bullets. It took all her strength to push the door shut—and all her courage to admit that she stood a better chance inside with the pirate than outside with the hurricane.

In a panic, she searched the house for something to use against him, something to provide protection in case he tried to attack her. Lord, he'd called her "lad." He wasn't just drunk, he was hallucinating, too. She nearly missed finding the coil of rope on the closet floor, until she tripped on it.

"That's it!" she cried. "I'll tie him up! So tight he won't be able to move. And once the storm dies down, I'll get the sheriff."

"Tie him up," Ben echoed. "Tie him up!"

By the time she finished, he looked like Gulliver after the Lilliputians were done with him. A riot of ropes circled his wrists and ankles, then wrapped around both his body and the couch. It would take superhuman strength to break the bonds and if she believed anything about this pirate, he would be too hung over to be sailing the high seas for some time.

Once he awoke, she'd question him, and if she decided it was safe to let him go, she would. If not, the sheriff could have him. As an added measure of protection, she retrieved a butcher knife from the kitchen before she curled into an overstuffed chair near the fireplace and watched him warily, exhausted.

Meredith closed her eyes and tipped her head back, trying to calm her racing heart. Suddenly, the raging weather outside didn't frighten her at all. This man had become her "Delia" now, the name she had given to all her fears since she'd been a child.

Meredith had been only eight years old when Hurricane Delia had roared along the Atlantic shore of the Outer Banks of North Carolina. She and her widowed father, a shrimp fisherman, had lived in a tiny weather-beaten cottage on the creek side of Ocracoke Village.

Though she had been only a child, her memories of that day had completely supplanted all the shining Christmas mornings and blurry birthday celebrations she'd come to experience in the following years. The day, September 11, 1976, had dawned calm and humid. But somewhere south of the island, Delia had lurked, turning the ocean into a terrifying force of nature. As darkness began to fall and the wind began to rise, her father had left her alone in their cottage, promising to return once he had checked the lines on his boat for a final time.

As he pulled on his rain suit and knee-high rubber boots, she had begged him to stay. He'd bent down from his towering height and told her she would be safe, tucked inside the house until he returned. But he hadn't returned. She'd crawled inside a dark closet and cried for her father, and then for her mother, even though Caroline Abbott was just a vague memory to her. She'd been left to face a hurricane alone and from that night on, Delia came back to haunt her dreams.

Her father had been injured that night and had nearly died, but with the help of friends on the island and Meredith's nursing, he'd recovered. His boat hadn't fared as well, but a bank loan repaired it and he continued to shrimp in the waters off the Outer Banks. Still, shrimping had been a hand-to-mouth existence before Delia, and it only got worse after the hurricane.

He lost his boat to the bank the year Meredith turned thirteen, bringing an end to her childhood on the island. Sam Abbott was forced to leave Ocracoke for a dredging job in Maryland, his young daughter in tow. How well she remembered that day, standing at the rail of the ferry and watching Ocracoke Island disappear behind the southern tip of Hatteras.

In her heart, she'd been secretly relieved. There would be no more dreams of Delia and no more hurricanes to fear. But though she hadn't missed Ocracoke, her father had. The island had been part of his blood, calling to him every minute he spent on the water. He died when Meredith was twenty-five, still longing to return to his island home.

So she had made the trip back for him, to bring back the memories of the times they'd spent together when she was young. And now, in less than a day, her life had turned into one major nightmare. She was trapped inside this cottage with a man who could very well be a psychopath.

But even though she knew she should be terrified, she wasn't. She was an adult. She had a big knife, an even bigger fireplace tool and a few more miles of rope if needed. She actually felt in control, as if she could handle whatever might happen.

And she could . . . until Ned the pirate decided to wake up.

HE WAS DEAD, of that much he was certain. He recalled very clearly falling overboard . . . or had he been pushed? God's teeth, his head ached. Had someone bashed him on the costard, as well? 'Twas no small talent for a man who had spent his entire life on the deck of a ship to simply pitch over the rail without cause. Aye, that must be the truth of it then. Murder had been done and Griffin Rourke had died of it.

But were he truly dead, he would not feel such blinding pain. If he were among the angels, he would have the power to open his eyes and look about, to know where he was. Unless his death had brought him to the devil's doorstep.

Griffin tried to move his arms and legs, but his limbs felt like lead ballast, too heavy to lift, as if he'd had a cup too much at the Horse and Plow. Then *that* be the truth of it. He was simply drunk and dreamed his trip into the brine. If he just opened his eyes, he'd find himself in his bed-chamber above the taproom, dragged there by the kindly innkeeper. Gathering his strength, he forced his eyelids open.

In a trice, he realized that he was neither dead nor drunk. He was trussed up like a Christmas goose and laid out on a huge settee in some strange parlor. And damned if someone hadn't shaved him, as well.

The room was lit by candles and lamps, hiding all detail deeply in the shadows. He slowly turned his head toward the flickering fire and his gaze came upon his captor. The boy slept, curled like a cream-fed cat in a chair that seemed to be fashioned of pillows. He was barely more than a child, smooth-faced and slender, with russet hair cropped above his ears. He wore an odd pair of breeches, made of indigo canvas, that reached his ankles, and a shirt that was many years too small for a boy of his age. He was a pretty lad, the kind who found easy favor with those debauched reprobates who eschewed the company of women.

Griffin opened his mouth to speak, then swallowed hard. His throat burned as if he'd been breathing saltwater. So he *had* gone overboard, and very nearly drowned by the taste of it. He licked his cracked lips and tried again.

"Boy," he croaked. "Boy!"

The lad sat up with a start. His eyes wide, he looked in Griffin's direction and then scrambled to retrieve a long blade he had hidden at his side. He stood, holding the knife out in front of him, watching Griffin with a wary eye.

"Put the blade away, boy," Griffin ordered, wincing at the pain that shot through his head. "I'm not of a mind to harm ye. Unless ye give me good cause. Now untie me, or face the consequences."

The boy shook his head, his eyes wide.

Griffin strained against the ropes and cursed. "By God, boy, you would do well not to anger me."

"I—I'm not going to untie you until you answer a few questions," the lad said, waving the knife in his direction. "Who are you? What is your name?"

The soft, sweet sound of the boy's voice was so unexpected that Griffin held his tongue and stared at his captor. Had his eyes been closed, he would have thought the voice belonged to a woman, full-grown. His gaze drifted down along the boy's slender body. Griffin groaned inwardly as he took in the tiny breasts, the narrow waist and the gentle swell of her hips.

"Damnation!" he muttered. He wished he had his fingers loose to rub away the ache in his temples. "I've been rendered helpless by a mere slip of a woman."

"Answer me!" she demanded. "Who are you?"

"Griffin Rourke," he muttered. "And who might you be, lass? Or is it, lad? Damn me, for I cannot settle on which it really is."

"Where are you from?"

"From?" Griffin snapped, glancing over at her. "You want to know where was I born?"

She nodded.

"I was born in the colony of Virginia on the James," he said tightly. "In my father's home in the room at the back of the house."

She glared at him. "You British still haven't gotten over the revolution, have you? Virginia is a state, not a colony. And you expect me to believe that you were born at home?"

"Where else?" Griffin asked. "Now, you must answer my questions. What is your name?"

"Meredith," she said. "Meredith Abbott."

He laughed harshly. "Then you *are* a boy."

"No!" she cried as if the observation caused insult.

"Yet, you carry a boy's name."

"Meredith is a girl's name, as well, and it has been for quite some time."

"What about your hair and clothing? Who allows you to dress like a lad?"

She seemed quite taken aback by his comments. "For your information, short hair is considered quite chic, and jeans are not the exclusive uniform for men. Just what planet have you been living on?"

"Planet? I do not understand," Griffin said. "How can I live on another planet? And what would you know of the planets? I have not met a woman yet who possesses a mind which can comprehend the complexities of Copernicus or Brahe or Kesler."

"Well, at least you don't think you're an alien life-form," Meredith said. "I guess we should be thankful for that. But you are the worst sort of male chauvinist, which isn't good. Why are you dressed like a pirate?"

"Damn it, girl, I'm done with this inquisition. Untie me!"

"No!" she retorted.

Griffin closed his eyes. "Then tell me where I am. And tell me when you plan to release me."

"You washed up on my beach during the storm and I dragged you into my cottage. You almost drowned, and would have if I hadn't saved you."

"You saved me?" he asked.

She nodded.

"Where? Where is this cottage you speak of?"

"On Loop Road on Ocracoke Island," she said.

"Occracock?" he asked. "I'm on Occracock? But I cannot be. There are no houses on Occracock."

"It's called Ocracoke," Meredith corrected. "And of course there are houses on the island. There's a whole village. There's been a village here for over two hundred years."

Griffin stared at her. She was mad, or bosky, or both. That was the only explanation for her holding him here. Or perhaps *he* was the one who had lost his mind. Who knows how long he had been tied up? He could have been unconscious for days.

"What is the date?" he asked.

She frowned. "September twenty-second."

He closed his eyes, relieved. He wasn't mad. The date *was* September twenty-second.

"Nineteen ninety-six," she added.

His eyes snapped open. "Nineteen ninety-six what?"

"That's the year," she said.

"You are mad," he murmured. "Untie me now, or I swear on my father's grave, I will kill you."

2

MEREDITH TIPPED her chin up defiantly, trying hard to maintain her composure over his blatant threat. "You're in no position to be threatening me," she said. "As soon as the storm breaks, I'm going to get the sheriff and he'll throw you in jail."

Griffin cursed and strained against the ropes. To Meredith's relief, the bonds showed no signs of weakening. All those childhood knot-tying lessons on her father's shrimp boat had finally proven useful.

When his tantrum seemed to have run its course, she walked over to the couch and looked down at him. "You're the one who put yourself in this mess, getting drunk, going out in the middle of a hurricane. Threatening to kill me isn't making matters better."

He ground his teeth. "I would not kill you," he said. "I am not a man who would harm a woman, even if she be a lunatic harpy. And I am not drunk, I'll have you know. It takes more than a finger of rum to put me in my cups."

"Then whatever possessed you to go out in the midst of a hurricane?"

"I did not," Griffin replied. "The sky was clear when I went overboard." He swore softly and frowned. "Yet I cannot perceive of how I came to be in the water."

"You mean to tell me, you fell off a boat?" Meredith asked. "Where?"

"We were sailing into Bath Town, ready to drop anchor in Old Town Creek. That is why you must untie me, lass. I have to deliver the purse before it is found missing."

She shook her head. Obviously the knock on his noggin had jostled his brain. Bath was over sixty miles away, on Bath Creek, not Old Town Creek, its name in colonial times. To end up on her beach, he would have had to float down Bath Creek into the Pamlico River and across Pamlico Sound, over sixty miles in the midst of a hurricane. Without a life jacket, he wouldn't have had a chance. Maybe it would be best to act as if she believed him. At least she might get more information to give the sheriff. "What purse?"

"It is tucked inside my waistcoat." He glanced down at his attire. "Where is my waistcoat?" he asked, his voice suddenly desperate.

Meredith stepped around the couch and fetched his vest, the odd garment she had tugged off his body before she hoisted him onto the couch. "There is no purse in here. You must have lost it when you went overboard. *If* you fell overboard, which I sincerely doubt you did."

"That cannot be so," he said. "I must find it." He strained against the ropes then cursed. "*You* must find it. For if he discovers it missing, he will not rest until he learns who has taken it. If he finds me missing, he will know."

Meredith shook her head. "I am not going back out in that storm. Besides, you could have dropped it anywhere. It could be floating in the Sound."

He stared at her, his blue gaze probing hers. "Take my hand," he said softly.

"No!"

"Take my hand," he repeated.

His deep voice was smooth and seductively persuasive. She watched him, wary of his motives, reluctant to touch him again. But his arms were pinned firmly to his sides by the ropes. Hesitantly, she did as she was told. His fingers were warm and strong and she felt an unbidden current of attraction as he squeezed her hand.

How long had it been since she'd been touched by a man? She tried to recall as his thumb softly stroked the back of her hand. But all her memories faded in the face of this man, this pirate. He possessed an incredible magnetism, a raw energy and power that could muddle her mind and drive her good sense right out the window.

"Upon my life," he urged softly, "I am not lying to you. I beg of you, you must find it, now, before it is too late."

Hypnotized by his gaze, she found herself nodding. Did she actually believe what he was saying? He seemed sincere, so much that she couldn't help thinking this purse of his meant a great deal. "All right," she said with a sigh. "I'll go out and search for it. What does it look like?"

"'Tis made of leather, tied in oiled canvas, the size of a small book."

Meredith grabbed her slicker and pulled it on. If she didn't know better, she'd think his mental state was rubbing off. She had to be crazy to go out into the storm again. "If I do this for you, you have to promise to behave until the sheriff gets here."

"I will," he said.

The wind had subsided considerably, but the rain spattered her face as she stepped outside. She held her hand to her forehead and made her way to the spot where she'd first found him, shining a flashlight in front of her. The beam struck something shiny and she bent down to pick it up. It was exactly as he had described it, a small packet, wrapped in waterproof canvas. Meredith tucked it into her pocket and ran to the house.

"The storm is weakening," she said as she stepped inside. Then she froze. Griffin was sitting up on the edge of the couch, methodically unwinding the ropes from around his ankles.

He glanced up at her and grinned. "You need not bother with the knife. I would disarm you in the blink of an eye, if you would try."

"You tricked me," she said, pressing her back against the door, ready to make her escape if she had to.

"'Tis always wise to let an enemy believe he—or she—has the upper hand. It makes him less vigilant." He gave her a sideways glance. "Ah, do not look so frightened, girl. I swore I would not harm ye and I am a man of my word."

"You didn't even care about this purse, did you?" Meredith accused. "It was just a ruse to get me out of the house."

He stood and tested his swollen knee. Meredith drew a sharp breath. She didn't realize until this moment how tall he was, well over six feet, his lithe body well-muscled and graceful. She watched as he ran his fingers through his shoulder-length hair, brushing it back from his face. He was a handsome man, a man who seemed to ooze danger from his very being. Yet, something told her she could trust him. He might be crazy, but she recognized a deep sense of honor in his character. He wouldn't hurt her.

"I have risked my life for that purse you hold," he said. "I would not treat it lightly." He held out his hand, but she refused to turn it over to him.

"You may look at it if you like," he offered.

With numb fingers, she untied the leather lace and unfolded the canvas. Inside a leather purse was a small book with a rough leather cover and a bundle of letters, some marked with sealing wax. To her surprise, all the documents were perfectly dry. She opened the book.

"It—it looks like an old journal," she said. "A logbook from a ship. My God, this must be quite a valuable antique. I can see why you were concerned."

He frowned. "An antique?"

She nodded as she continued to scan the entries. "How old is it?"

"Old? 'Tis not old at all."

"What year was it written?"

"It begins nearly a year ago, in 1717. I suppose I will have to trust you, Merrie-girl, though I do not know why. What you hold in your hand is the evidence I need against the devil himself."

"The devil?" Meredith asked.

"Teach," he muttered. "The pirate Blackbeard."

Meredith stared at him, openmouthed, then looked down at the journal. His words whirled in her mind. She slowly flipped through the pages, now reading the text more closely. The entries recounted nautical positions and weather conditions, all in a spidery hand reminiscent of colonial times. There were also long lists of what appeared to be captured booty. She recognized many of the names contained within—Israel Hands, the first mate . . . and the boatswain Gibbens, the quartermaster Miller, Curtice, Jackson, and more.

"Are you telling me this is Edward Teach's journal?" she asked in disbelief.

He nodded. "Aye. And there is correspondence as well that proves Teach is in league with Eden, the governor of North Carolina. I stole them from Teach's cabin and have to deliver them to Spotswood's man tonight and then return them again before the *Adventure* sets sail. 'Tis the proof that's needed to bring the pirate down. He will be hanged for this."

Meredith shook her head and held up her hand. "Stop. Right now. Who put you up to this? I'll bet it was Katherine Conrad, wasn't it? She'd do anything to mess up my chances at winning the Sullivan Fellowship. She thinks they'll name *her* department head after Dr. Moore retires, but *I'm* going to get the post. How much did she pay you to forge an original source?"

Griffin lifted his left eyebrow and looked at her as if she'd just told him there were Martians living in her refrigerator. He shrugged warily. "She did not pay me a farthing," he replied slowly.

He was obviously not quite sure how to phrase his answer to please her. He thought she was as crazy as she believed *him* to be. Meredith closed her eyes and drew a deep breath, trying to organize her thoughts. The notion was preposterous at best, yet she couldn't deny it. She held the very proof in her hands, original documents, signatures and handwriting that she'd seen with her own eyes in museums and archives. She knew Blackbeard's life better than she knew her own and she could not dispute the credibility of these documents. Either they were authentic, or someone had spent a great deal of time and money on fakes.

There had always been rumors of Blackbeard's keeping a journal, of letters that had given solid proof of the pirate's arrangement with the governor of North Carolina, Charles Eden, the man who shared in the pirate's loot in return for protection from the law. But somewhere along the way, the letters had been lost. Now, if this man was telling the truth, she held them in her hand.

Meredith quelled a violent shiver. For her to believe these documents were real, she would also have to believe something even more preposterous. She would have to believe that this man, this Griffin Rourke, with his handmade boots and his odd way of speaking, had somehow traveled through time to bring her these papers.

She stood and tossed the leather pouch on the coffee table. "I don't believe this. It can't be possible. These are forgeries and *you* are a fraud."

"Believe what you will," he said. "I do not care. Now, do you possess a horse?"

Meredith stared up at him distractedly. "We're on Ocracoke Island. What good will a horse do you?"

He opened his mouth to speak, then schooled his expression into blandness. She understood the look. He didn't believe they were on Ocracoke Island, either. "Don't look at me like that!" she cried.

"Like what?"

She rubbed her forehead. "Like you don't believe what I'm saying. Just stop this charade and tell me who you really are!"

"I have told you, girl. Would have me say it all again?"

"Stop it!"

He chuckled and shook his head. "All right, Merrie, my girl, I will believe whatever you will have me believe, as long as you find me a good horse and forget you ever met me."

She slowly approached him and sat down on the couch, staring into his eyes. "You aren't lying, are you?"

"No," he replied.

She buried her face in her hands and turned away from him, unable to look at him any longer. "Oh, God, I *am* going crazy. This hurricane has sent me right over the edge. There's just no way... no way... it just isn't possible. I have to be dreaming, that's the only explanation."

He stepped in front of her and pried her fingers off her eyes. "The horse, Merrie. I need a horse."

Merrie avoided his gaze, logic at war with reality, the battle jangling her nerves and muddling her mind until she could not think straight. She drew a deep breath, then spoke the words, words she didn't really believe, but words that had to be said. "Griffin, I want you to listen to me very carefully and answer truthfully. Do you consider yourself an open-minded man?"

He reached out and cupped her chin in his hand, drawing her gaze up to meet his pale, wary eyes. She felt a flood of warmth rush through her body as their eyes locked and she didn't pull away. His touch didn't frighten her. Instead, it seemed to calm her, to prove that he was a real man and not just a figment of her imagination.

"I do not understand," he said softly, his brow furrowed with concern. "Open-minded?"

"A—a freethinker," she amended. "Do you consider yourself a freethinker?"

"Yes," he said. "I do."

"And what about science? Do you believe there are many things yet to be explained in our world, many things that will become clear to future generations?"

He nodded solemnly. "I would have to agree with that theory," Griffin said.

Meredith drew a steadying breath and pushed ahead. "Then I want you to consider the fact that you might not belong here. That you might have—" She closed her eyes and shook her head. "I can't believe I'm about to say this." She opened her eyes, then reached up and grabbed his hand from her face, squeezing it hard. "That you might have somehow stepped through . . . I don't know what to call it . . . a door in time."

He nodded indulgently, drawing away from her before picking up his boots. He winced as he pulled the left boot up to his swollen knee. "Of course, Merrie, I think that may be very likely. A quite proper theory, if I do say so myself. You are a very clever girl."

"I'm not insane, Griffin, so please don't treat me like I am. I am dead serious here."

Griffin chuckled, tugged on his other boot, then retrieved his tattered waistcoat. "Of that I am sure. Now, I must take my leave." He grabbed the pouch from the coffee table and retied the leather thong around the canvas, then tucked it inside his waistcoat.

"You can't go out there," Meredith said, grabbing his hand.

He grasped her shoulders gently, sending another rush of warmth through her limbs. "The storm is nearly over," he murmured. "Do not worry yourself. I will be safe. I have faced much worse and lived to tell the tale."

Meredith stared up into his eyes, eyes that in such a short time had become intimately familiar to her. How could she convince him of what she believed? How could she tell him that he'd been kidnapped from his task and dropped into the twentieth century?

"You saved my life, Merrie. I will not forget ye." He bent down and kissed her gently on the cheek. The touch of his firm lips on her skin sent a frisson of desire straight to her core. She felt her knees wobble slightly and her breath catch in her throat. Hesitantly, she reached up to place her hands on his chest, but then he was gone, heading toward the door.

"Wait!" she cried. "I have to show you something before you leave."

He forced a smile and walked back to the couch. "What is it, Merrie?"

Frantically, she searched the dimly lit room for something, anything that might prove her theory. If the electricity were working, she could show him any number of things—the television, the microwave, the lights. But without electricity...

Her gaze stopped on the can of shaving cream that still sat on the coffee table. "Hold out your hand," she ordered.

He frowned, but did as he was told. She pushed the button on the can and white foam exploded from the nozzle. He snatched his hand away then shook the foam from it. "It's shaving cream," she said. "Watch." She shook the can again and began to build a mound of lime-scented foam in her own hand. "It's an aerosol can. Look at it, Griffin. All this foam out of such a tiny can. Do you have this where you come from? Do you even have tin cans?"

He backed away, his expression leery, but she followed him, wiping the foam from her hand and snatching the flashlight. She flipped it on and shined it in his eyes. "And this? Light with the push of a button. See, there's no flame." Meredith laughed. "You don't even have electricity yet. Benjamin Franklin is just a boy. He hasn't even thought of experimenting with a kite and a key." She pushed the flashlight into his grip and showed him how it worked, but as soon as she let go, he threw it to the floor as if it had burned his hand.

"You are a witch," he said.

She grabbed him by the hands. "Look at me. Look at the way I'm dressed. Do you recognize clothes like these? My name is Meredith Elizabeth Abbott. I was born on March nineteenth, 1968. Nineteen sixty-eight," she repeated more slowly. "Almost three hundred years *after* you. And outside is a whole new world, a world with cars and planes and computers. We're no longer part of the British Empire, we're a nation that stretches from one coast to another. We've fought a war for our independence and won, and we fought a war against each other that tore this country in two. Griffin, we landed a man on the moon more than twenty-five years ago."

He disentangled his fingers from hers and slowly backed toward the door. "For your own safety, Merrie, I would not repeat these words to another soul. There are some that might burn you at the stake for such heresy."

"Griffin, please, don't go out there. Not until you understand what's waiting. Not until you believe me."

He grabbed the doorknob and opened the door. The cold, damp wind blew in around him, whipping his long dark hair around his face and making the wide sleeves of his linen shirt flutter.

Their gazes met for a long moment, his blue eyes piercing to the very center of her soul, and she knew he didn't believe her. And then, he stepped through the door and closed it behind him.

Meredith stood frozen in place, unable to think of anything more she might say to him. She tipped her head back and sighed. He would have to learn on his own, see the world with his own eyes. He couldn't go far. They were on an island that was only sixteen miles long and a mile wide, and the ferries wouldn't start running again until the seas had calmed.

If he came to believe her, he would be back, and if he didn't . . . well, if he didn't, there was nothing more she could do for him. Meredith rubbed her eyes, then turned and walked to the bedroom. It was nearly three in the morning and she'd been awake for almost twenty-four hours. The storm had quieted enough for her to sleep now.

As she crawled into the bed and pulled the covers up to her chin, she tried to quiet her frenzied thoughts, tried to put all that had transpired out of her mind. She pulled the pillow over her face and practiced a relaxation technique she'd learned in a meditation class. Slowly, she felt herself drifting off, slipping into sleep by degrees.

Sometime in the early morning, just after the sun came up, she woke with a start. Pushing herself up, Meredith looked around the room in confusion. The gentle roar of the waves and the sound of blue jays in the trees told her that the storm had finally passed.

Her muddled mind flashed an image of a man with long dark hair and a perfect profile, dressed like a pirate. Meredith groaned and punched her pillow, then flopped back down. She had dreamed the dream again, only this time, it had seemed so real, so vivid she could recall nearly every detail as if she'd actually lived it.

"Go to sleep, Dorothy," she muttered to herself. "You're back in Kansas, now, safe and sound."

THE NOONDAY SUN filtered through the lace curtains of the bedroom window. Meredith squinted against the light and yawned. With a soft moan, she stretched, throwing her arm out to the side. But instead of hitting the mattress, her hand came to rest on something hard and warm and very muscular. She turned her head and noticed a man's leg.

Levering herself up, she screamed. A hand clamped over her mouth. "'Tis me, Merrie. Do not be afraid."

She looked up into familiar blue eyes, eyes that she thought she'd seen in a dream, eyes that were ringed with red and filled with exhaustion. He sat on the edge of the bed, facing her, his hair wild and windblown. She swallowed hard and he slowly pulled his hand from her lips, leaving a warm, tingling imprint where he had touched her.

"Griffin?" she whispered. Hesitantly, she reached out and touched his face to be certain he was real.

He stared at her, long and hard, his expression etched with confusion. "I believe you," he said softly. He slowly wrapped his arms around her waist and lowered his head to her lap, then closed his eyes. "I believe you. Now find a way for me to return."

Meredith hesitantly reached out and stroked his hair, hoping to offer some comfort. The long strands slipped through her shaky fingers like fine silk. Her fingertips brushed against his temple and she let them rest there for a moment, enjoying the warmth of his skin, feeling his slow, strong pulse.

"I should have believed you, but I thought..." He paused and drew a ragged breath. "I thought you were mad. And now, I am beginning to believe I am the one who has lost all sense of things."

"I know how you feel," she said as she gently brushed a raven strand from his cheek. "Believe me, I understand. But there is no other explanation." She felt his tension abate, his coiled muscles relax, and she listened as his breathing grew soft and even, calmer.

She hadn't dreamed him. He was real and he was here, caught in a time and place where he didn't belong. Why she believed it all, she didn't really know. She'd taken an incredible leap of faith, believed in a concept that most academicians would find improbable, if not downright impossible.

But she *did* believe and that was all that really mattered. Somehow, he'd crossed a bridge, turned a corner, opened a door and stepped through. Fate, or destiny, or some force greater than both of them had brought him here, to Ocracoke and to her. And now, a strange man lay in her bed, yet she felt not a trace of insecurity or apprehension.

He wasn't here to seduce her. In fact, she suspected what he was feeling right now was paralyzing fear. He clung to her, his face buried against her stomach as if she was the only familiar thing in this unfamiliar world. Strange, how such a fierce man could suddenly reveal such a vulnerable side of himself. Meredith moved her fingers to his forehead, smoothing the hair away from his brow.

It felt so natural to touch him, as if they'd known each other forever. Yet, she knew that wasn't true. They barely knew each other at all. But they did share an astounding secret and in that, they became unwitting companions, confidants, strangers who had no one else but each other to cling to while they untangled the mysteries of his trip through time.

"Why am I here?" he said.

"I don't know," Meredith replied. She searched her mind for an explanation, any explanation. As she ran the situation around in her mind, a slow, sick feeling gripped her stomach.

Oh, Lord, maybe it wasn't fate that had brought him here. Maybe it was *her* fault! Meredith sank back into the pillows and stared at the ceiling, unable to untangle what had happened in the past twelve hours. So maybe she did have occasional fantasies about pirates. That certainly didn't mean she'd summoned this man out of his own time and into the twentieth century.

Discounting that explanation, another came quickly to mind. Maybe she'd brought him here for professional reasons, to help with her work on Blackbeard. It seemed more than a coincidence that he was spying on the same man she was studying. The Sullivan Fellowship had become an all-consuming dream, but it was just that, a dream.

Was she really the one who'd caused this man such un-happiness? Had she somehow played God with his life and brought him here for her own selfish reasons?

"I've never seen anything like it," he murmured.

She looked down to find his eyes open and fixed on her face. He pushed up and braced his head on his elbow. His fingers toyed at a button on her nightshirt.

"Wha—what?" she stammered, realizing how close his fingers were to the bare skin above her breasts.

"I'm not sure what it was. It was like a carriage without horses. It moved under its own power. I looked for the sails, but I could not find them."

"It—it's called an automobile," she explained, pushing back a wave of guilt. "It was invented by Henry Ford in 1903. An engine makes it go, but don't ask me how. The internal workings of a car remains a mystery to most people."

"Have you ever ridden in a carriage like this?"

"I own one, but I left it on the mainland when I came here. Most people own their own car. There are some places in this country where there are roads that are six lanes across and cars travel very fast."

"How fast?"

"Seventy miles an hour."

Griffin frowned in disbelief. "Does this not harm a person, traveling at such a speed? Would his limbs not be torn from his body?"

"No," Meredith said. "We have airplanes that travel much—" She paused. There was no reason to tell him more. "Never mind."

He sat up and stared into her eyes. "I don't belong here," he said.

She nodded. "I know."

"I must return and finish what I have started."

"Do you mean Blackbeard?"

"I made a vow on my father's grave that I would avenge his death. Teach robbed me of my father. I plan to make him pay for that crime and all his others."

"How?" Meredith asked.

"I sail on Teach's ship, the *Adventure*," Griffin said. "I believe they would call me a spy. I work for Spotswood, the governor of Virginia. Like me, he is determined to bring the pirate down. The contents of the purse are the proof we need to bring action against Teach, to raise a force and capture him. He will be hung for his crimes and I will be there to see it done."

"I—I know a little bit about Blackbeard," Meredith explained, not willing to tell him everything. If her connection to Blackbeard was part of the reason he was here, she couldn't tell him. He'd only blame her. She'd have to find a way to return him to his own time, and then maybe she could tell him about her work. "I teach history at the College of William and Mary. I'm considered an expert in American maritime history."

He frowned. "*You* teach at William and Mary?"

She pushed herself up and turned to him, crossing her legs and resting her elbows on her knees. "Yes, me, a woman. In this day and age, women are considered equal to men. We have the same educational opportunities, we hold important jobs. I have a doctoral degree in history."

"William and Mary is for men, not women."

Meredith grinned. "Not anymore."

"So what do you know of Teach?"

She smiled. "He's probably the most famous pirate of all time. Everyone has heard of Blackbeard."

"And did he live a long life?"

"Blackbeard was killed on Friday, November twenty-second, 1718, when two ships under the command of

Lieutenant Robert Maynard and under the orders of Governor Alexander Spotswood of Virginia attacked the pirate in Ocracoke Inlet. The battle happened in the waters just beyond the back door of this cottage."

Griffin rolled onto his back and threw his arm over his eyes. "It will be done then, with or without me. My father's death will be avenged."

Meredith bit her lower lip and winced. "I don't think we can be sure of that now."

He sat up and stared at her, a deep scowl creasing his forehead. "Explain, please."

She drew a deep breath and tried to remember her science fiction. "There is a theory that says that events in history are . . . very fragile." She struggled to explain. "Think of time as a brick wall, course after course laid on top of each other but without mortar. If you remove one brick, the wall might fall, or it might not, depending upon how important the brick is. You're a brick in Blackbeard's wall," Meredith explained. "If you're not there to play your part, he may not fall."

"You have these—these automobiles that travel very fast. You say that a man has voyaged to the moon. So you must have a conveyance to send me back to my time."

A long silence grew between them.

"You *do* know the way, do you not?" Griffin asked.

"Griffin, we can cross the Atlantic in a few hours on a supersonic airplane, but I'm afraid we haven't yet invented a machine that can travel through time. But that doesn't mean there isn't a way. We just have to figure out how you got here. Once we do that, we'll be able to figure out how to send you back."

"We don't have much time, Merrie-girl," he said, exhaustion tinging his voice.

"No," Meredith replied. "We don't."

She reached out and placed her palm on his beard-roughened cheek, giving him a tremulous smile. He leaned close then drew her into his arms. They clung to each other for a long time, silent, taking solace in each other's touch.

How much she'd come to care for Griffin and in such a short time. Was it merely because she might be at the root of all his problems? Or was it more? Had her secret fantasies of pirates suddenly taken on human form? Whatever these strange feelings might be, she knew she had to help him—she owed him that much.

"It will be all right," she said softly.

Slowly, he dragged her down into the bed, pulling her against his body, curling himself along her back and snuggling his chin against her shoulder. Eyes wide with shock, she lay next to him, afraid to move, not quite certain what he expected of her.

His warm breath teased at her ear and she listened as his breath grew soft and even. When he finally slept, she realized that she'd been foolish to think he wanted more from her. He was simply a man out of time, confused by all that had happened to him and in need of the comfort of another human being. He needed her for as long as he remained here, and she would be there for him, until they said their goodbyes.

As she let herself drift off to sleep, his muscled body pressed against hers, she realized that saying goodbye to a man like Griffin Rourke might be harder than she ever imagined.

GRIFFIN STOOD on the narrow strip of sand behind the cottage, staring out at the water. Wispy clouds scudded across the sky, pushed along by the same brisk breeze that capped the waves with white. If he watched the water long enough, he could almost forget the strange place he'd come to and believe he was back home.

This sea had carried him from one century to another for a reason he had yet to comprehend. Maybe it held the answer to his return. He was tempted to walk into the surf, to let the waves cover his head, to breathe in the saltwater and let his body drift away on the current. But would it carry him back the way he came?

As if God was playing a foul trick on him, he had been snatched from his purpose and dropped here. There had been times when he'd wished for his own death, first when he'd been riddled with guilt after Jane and the baby had been taken by the fever while he was at sea. Then, when he had taken to drink to soothe his sorrow.

But after his father's untimely death, only revenge would do. His friends had claimed that to be a spy on Teach's ship was as much suicide as courage. But this place was not the noble death he had imagined, but merely a hellish exile where he would remain powerless to complete his plan.

Yet within this hell lived an angel. Merrie, his guardian, his rescuer. She was an odd girl, but then perhaps not so odd for this time. She was not what the gossips of his time would consider beautiful. But she was slender and graceful and strangely exotic to his own eyes. She had cropped her dark hair, yet it did not detract from her looks but enhanced them, drawing the eye to her face, to that smooth, ivory skin like the finest porcelain, unmarked by age or disease or dissipation.

But beyond her looks, there was something else. She was a quick and clever girl, well-spoken, educated and independent, not the kind that a man might want for a wife, but a woman who might provide a welcome diversion from the ordinary.

His mind wandered back to the feel of her body pressed against his. He had been a long time without a woman, over a year of self-imposed celibacy. He had dishonored Jane after her death by crawling inside a whiskey bottle and every warm and willing wench he encountered. When he finally pulled himself out, he'd vowed to be pure and chaste until such time as another woman, worthy of Jane's memory, came along.

Merrie was not that woman, but she could certainly test his resolve. As he had watched her sleep, he'd imagined having her. She had all but offered herself to him, allowing him to lie beside her in her bed, to spend the night in her house.

That his angel was fallen should make no difference to him, but it did. He wanted to believe her to be pure and untouched, but he knew she wasn't. She lived in this cottage alone, banished to this island by a society that could not accept her behavior and her mode of dress. He wondered what had led to her fall. Had she loved a man who had despoiled her and then deserted her?

Griffin sat down in the grass, digging his bare toes into the damp strip of sand along the water's edge. He could offer to kill the man for her, to demand satisfaction in a duel. He was considered an excellent shot and a cool head with a sword. It would be the least he could do in return for her saving his life.

A hand touched his shoulder and he looked up to find Merrie's smiling face. "I was wondering if you were hungry," she said. "The electricity came back on, so I could cook something. You haven't eaten since . . . since you got here."

Griffin patted the grass beside him and she sat down.

"I could not help noticing that you are a plainspoken woman, Merrie. You speak your mind in a forthright manner. I would ask you a question."

She wrapped her arms around her knees and shrugged. "Ask away. But I told you all I know about automobiles."

"That is not what I would ask. I want to know if it is a man who has brought you to this place?"

She frowned. "No. I came on the ferry."

Griffin bit back a curse. He was not making himself clear, yet he knew no other delicate way to put it. He decided to change his tack. "Would it be best for me to leave here, before my presence is known and tongues begin to wag? You have helped me, Merrie, and I don't wish to bring more harm to your reputation."

"You don't have to leave. You can stay here while we try to figure this thing out."

"Then that is the way of it?" he said, frowning. "You would have me live here with you? To *be* with you?"

"We're adults, Griffin, and we don't need to answer to anyone."

He paused, turning his eyes out to sea as he took in her blunt statement. Did she mean for them to become lovers, then? Was she offering herself to him? He'd met many women of questionable morals in his life, but none more sweet and lovely than Merrie. And the thought that he might take her, here and now, with no protest from her lips, stirred raw desire deep inside of him.

But something held him back. He owed Merrie his life. To take her out of lust would dishonor her—and him. He would not surrender to his instincts, he vowed. Not now, not yet. Still, as he turned to look at her again, he knew that to resist her would be difficult. Especially since she seemed willing.

"How old are you?" Griffin asked.

"I'm twenty-eight, nearly twenty-nine," Merrie said.

"And you have not married?"

"No," she said, a touch of defensiveness in her voice. "I'm still young. And I've been too busy with my career."

"Then you have a protector? A benefactor who keeps you?"

"What?" Merrie gasped. "No! I keep myself!"

Griffin cursed inwardly. He was not handling this well at all. Though they spoke the same language, he was at sixes and sevens, as if he were expressing himself in Latin or Greek. "Are you considered worthy of respect in this village, even though you invite the company of men into your home without others present?" Now, her expression showed anger and he knew he'd made a hash of things.

"Griffin, I'm going to give you one piece of advice while you're here and I want to you take it to heart. Loosen up. Things have changed. A lot."

"Loosen up," Griffin repeated. "And what might this mean?"

"It means, relax. If you wanted to, you could dress up in ladies' clothes and walk down Main Street and a lot of folks wouldn't give you a second look."

He shifted uncomfortably, not certain what she was implying. "Why would I want to do this?"

"I don't know. The important thing is, you *can*, and nobody will arrest you for it. They may even find it entertaining."

Griffin tried to imagine such a thing, but couldn't. He decided the conversation had strayed well off the path of his original intent. "So, there is no man that you would have me challenge for your honor?"

"You mean like fight a duel?"

Griffin nodded.

Merrie pushed to her feet and walked to the water, letting the gentle waves lap at her bare feet. She turned to look at him, her smile quirking as if she was about to burst into fits of laughter. "Thank you for the offer, and I'll keep it in mind, but right now I can't think of a soul I'd want you to kill for me."

He joined her at the water's edge and grabbed her hand. "So what are we to do next, if you have no one I might shoot?"

"As soon as the phone is working again, I thought I would call a friend of mine. Kelsey is a physics professor at William and Mary."

"She is a physician?"

"No. She's a physicist. She studies electrons and gravity and about a million other things I really don't understand. If she doesn't know about time-travel theory, she will know where to send us."

"Then we must leave today," Griffin said, trying to control his excitement. "Will we travel by water or by land? Is the college still in the same place as it was in my time? If it is, I vow it would be faster to travel by water. If the wind is with us, it will take us less than a week's time."

"The college is still in Williamsburg. But we don't have to go there. We can just call her . . . on the telephone." Merrie sighed. "Why don't we have lunch and I'll explain the telephone over toasted cheese sandwiches. After that, I want to go downtown and pick up some clothes for you. If you expect to walk around the island during the day, it would be best if you fit in."

"So there is something wrong with my clothes?" he asked. "They are serviceable garments."

"They're just not quite the rage in this day and age," she said.

"I will not wear a dress," Griffin countered. "I am not that . . . loose."

Merrie giggled, a warm, musical sound that filled his senses. "Relax. Men in the twentieth century aren't expected to wear ladies' dresses. They just can if they want to."

"Well, I do not want to," Griffin said firmly.

She grinned, her smile teasing and sweet. "I never had any doubt about that, Griffin Rourke."

3

"I CANNOT WEAR these garments! I will look the fool!"

Meredith stood outside the bathroom door, her shoulder braced on the wall. "The clothes are fine, Griffin. You can't walk around in that pirate outfit. People will stare. Now get dressed, we're in a hurry."

The door flew open and Griffin stood in front of her, dressed only in a pair of boxer shorts. "They will stare if I wear this. I would not show my knees in public!"

A laugh escaped Meredith's throat. She pressed her fingers to her lips. Finding underwear for Griffin had been the most difficult of her shopping tasks on the island. Most people shopped on the mainland or at the mall in Nags Head for their essentials. But barring a long shopping trip, she'd been forced to settle for the silk boxers she'd found at a local souvenir shop. The fabric was decorated with little buccaneer's heads, each one complete with eye patch, tricorn and dagger clenched between teeth.

Her gaze wandered the length of his body and she felt a delicious shiver skitter up her spine. Griffin had an incredible physique, a body any woman would find attractive. His legs were long and muscular, and the boxer shorts only seemed to enhance his flat belly and narrow waist. His broad chest was tanned golden brown, and for an instant she could imagine him on the deck of a ship, the sun beating down on his skin, the salt breeze whipping his dark hair around his face.

For a moment, she was tempted to tell him that if he expected to live in the twentieth century, he would have to wear boxer shorts twenty-four hours a day. But he seemed so upset by the prospect that she reluctantly decided to tell him the truth.

"You're wearing underwear," Meredith explained. "I bought you several pairs of pants. You put those on *over* the underwear."

Frowning, Griffin stepped back into the bathroom and emerged a few minutes later with a pair of khaki cotton pants he'd pulled from a bag. He held them up against his waist and examined them, then tugged them on in front of her as if dressing in front of a female caused him no embarrassment at all.

"Feel better?" she asked.

"I feel warmer, at least," he said. "What is this?" He stared down at the zipper in confusion. "There are no buttons here."

"That's a zipper," Meredith said. "Just tug up on that little tab."

He fumbled with the zipper. "I cannot. You do this for me." He braced his hands on his hips and waited.

Meredith's eyes widened. "You can do it," she urged, twisting her fingers in front of her and giving him an encouraging smile.

"I cannot," he repeated in frustration. "Show me."

With shaking hands, Meredith hesitantly reached out and plucked at the tab of the zipper. If she knew how to swoon, she would have done it then and there. But she'd never fainted in her life. Biting at her bottom lip, she slowly closed the zipper, trying not to think about what was on the other side.

He watched her in amazement. "How does this work?"

She snatched her hands away. "Little teeth," she muttered. "Now put your shirt on so we can go. I've got the computer reserved at the library. I want to hop on the Net and see what I can find out about time travel."

He stared at her for a long moment, then shrugged and returned to the bathroom.

Ten minutes later, she and Griffin were headed down Lighthouse Road to the tiny island library behind the fire hall. Though his presence at her side caused a few curious stares from the locals, no one was nosy enough to ask what their relationship was. And she didn't volunteer any information, except that he was a friend who had come for a short visit. Tourists were not uncommon on Ocracoke, even in the fall, and most of the townsfolk appeared to accept him with little notice.

As they walked, he asked questions about everything and anything—about the quaint lighthouse that stood sentinel over the Sound and the picturesque cottages and shops that dotted the narrow streets. They took the long loop to the library, along the waterfront and then down the narrow street that led to the tiny cemetery that held the bodies of four British sailors. The sailors' ship had been torpedoed offshore by a German U-boat during the Second World War. Griffin wasn't satisfied until she recited everything she knew about the country's involvement in the war and the current state of the U.S. Navy.

"Why are we going to the library?" he asked.

"I told you. I want to get on the Net and see what I can learn about time travel. My laptop doesn't have a modem so we have to use the computer at the library."

"The Net," he repeated.

"Internet," she explained. "It's a computer network."

"Computer," he repeated.

"You'll see," she said, patting him on the shoulder. Meredith stepped to the edge of the road, ready to cross, when Griffin grabbed her arm.

"Have a care," he warned, staring at a car nearly a block away. She had noticed that he'd become watchful, wary, as if he wasn't quite sure about the intentions of the automobiles or their drivers. He slipped his arm protectively around her waist and a flood of warmth rushed through her at his touch.

She knew she was growing fond of him. He was a strong and vital man with a powerful sensual appeal. She had to keep from watching him, admiring the way he moved, the way his skin gleamed in the sun, the way he stared out at the water with pale hooded eyes. And every time he touched her, her heart quickened and her breathing stopped.

She'd never felt so comfortable around a man as she felt with Griffin. He seemed to accept her for exactly who she was. All her insecurities and inexperience with men didn't seem to matter. In fact, he considered her a fallen woman simply for allowing him to stay in her house.

But then, maybe she *was* a fallen woman, at least by his standards. She had gone to bed with five different men in her life, fully intending to lose her virginity, right up until the very moment of truth. But then, the whole thing had seemed wrong and she had put an end to it, leaving her partners confused and sometimes even angry.

When it came right down to it, only one thing kept her from ridding herself of her virtue. She wasn't in love. And something deep inside her soul told her to wait—for a man to whom she might give her heart as well as her body. So she'd waited. And she was still waiting . . .

Meredith stepped inside the library with Griffin at her heels. She smiled at the volunteer librarian, Tank Muldoon's sister, Trina, then headed for the computer in the corner. Griffin lingered for a long moment as he passed the shelves of books.

"Whose books are these?" he asked.

"They belong to the community," Meredith answered distractedly as she signed on to the computer. "They're for everyone. This is a public library."

"And we will find our answers in these books?" he said.

"No," Meredith said. "I doubt that there are any books here that will help us."

He sat down beside her and peered at the computer screen. "I thought you said we were seeking information about sending me back. Why are you looking into this box?" he demanded. "There are many books here which would help us. We must look at them."

Meredith sighed. "This box is a computer, Griffin, and there's more information in here than in a thousand libraries this size."

Griffin scoffed in disbelief, then slouched down in his chair like a petulant child. "This I don't believe. You are wasting time."

She could already hear the impatience growing in his voice and she knew he was about to fall into one of his dark moods. He'd been with her just a day and a half and already she could read him as if she'd known him for years.

Last night, he had paced the night away, impatiently covering every inch of the floor like a caged tiger. From her bed, she had heard him prowling around the cottage, muttering to himself and sometimes to Ben Gunn, keeping the leather purse always close at hand, as if he was worried he might be swept away at any moment.

This morning, he had been preoccupied, his mind firmly focused in the past, on Edward Teach—which was exactly where her mind should have been focused, too. She wanted to talk to him of his life, to learn everything he knew about Blackbeard. Though she wouldn't be able to use most of it in her book without an original source to back up what he told her, it would give her work new insight into the famous pirate. Still, something held her back from telling him about her work.

What was it? Was she afraid he might suspect what she suspected—that *she* was somehow responsible for bringing him here? Every time she looked at him, she felt the same nagging sense of guilt. And every impulse she had to broach the subject of the pirate was buried beneath that guilt.

"When is this friend of yours going to call?"

Meredith glanced over at him and forced a smile, hoping to defuse his mood. "I told you, Kelsey is attending a symposium at Wake Forest," she explained. "She'll call as soon as she returns. Maybe tomorrow or the next day."

"And you are certain this Kelsey will be able to find a way for me to go back?"

"I don't know," Meredith replied. "Griffin, I won't get anything done if you keep talking to me. This takes concentration. It's like navigating a boat."

He stood up and began to pace the floor behind her. "I feel so damn useless here," he muttered. "I am not accustomed to idleness. I need to do something."

"In this century, we place great value on our leisure time," Meredith commented lightly. "That's why people visit this island, for the laid-back life-style."

He stopped suddenly and stared down at her. "Well, I am not from this century, am I?" he replied, his voice dripping with sarcasm. With that, he turned and stalked toward the door, yanking it open before he stepped outside.

With a soft curse, Meredith pushed herself back from the computer and stood, shooting an apologetic smile to a wide-eyed Trina. She found Griffin outside where he'd taken up pacing the sidewalk. She grabbed his elbow and drew him to a stop. "Griffin, I'm doing everything I can to help you. But you have to be patient. This is very complicated."

He stared at her for a moment, anger blazing in his gaze. Then, with a resigned sigh, he closed his eyes and raked his fingers through his hair, schooling his temper. "Forgive me. I did not mean to speak so harshly."

"I understand," Meredith said. She paused, then looked up at him hopefully. "I was thinking that maybe you'd enjoy a trip to Bath, or Bath Town, as you call it. I can borrow a car and we can take the ferry across to Swan Quarter early tomorrow morning. You can tell me all about how the town used to be. You can show me where Blackbeard had his house."

"To what end?" he muttered.

"I—I just thought it might—"

"Occupy my mind?" he completed. "I don't need my mind filled with trivial matters. I have plenty to do. I was to deliver the purse to Spotswood's man before I returned to sail with the *Adventure*. But while I am here, the work goes on without me. How am I to know whether they are proceeding?"

She slipped her arm through his and paced alongside him. "Well, there is a theory that would have us believe that if history is altered, the books written about the event will also change. So, I suppose we could just look at the books that have been written about Blackbeard and see if they've changed."

"Whose theory is this?"

"I'm not sure. I saw it in a movie called *Back to the Future*," she said.

"A movie?"

"A video," Meredith said. "It's like a play you watch on . . . well, just think of it as a play."

"Ah," he said, nodding. "And this video was written by a respected scholar, an expert in this science . . . this physics, like your colleague, Kelsey?"

"No, not exactly. Movies and videos are entertainment. They're fuel for the imagination. Even though there are plenty of books and movies about the subject, no one has ever really traveled in time."

He stopped short and spun her around to face him. "No one?"

A tremor raced through her at the look in his eyes and she bit her bottom lip. "I—I thought you understood that. As far as I know, no one has ever traveled in time."

A myriad of emotions crossed his face before he spoke again. "Then I am the first," he stated softly. "And I must be the first to return, as well."

Meredith drew a deep breath and screwed up her courage to say the words she'd wanted to say since he'd come to her. Words she knew would anger him. "What if you can't get back?" she asked.

"I will not consider that possibility," he said. "I must return."

She swallowed hard. "Is—is there someone waiting for you?" She felt her cheeks flame. "I mean, do you have a girlfriend . . . or maybe a fiancée . . . or a wife?"

Meredith risked a glance up. He was staring up at the sky, his gaze fixed on some invisible star. His eyes were frosted with pain and his thoughts had drifted to a different time. She'd never seen such a look on a person's face, such intense anguish, so tightly controlled yet so visible.

She wanted to reach out and pull him into her arms to comfort him. But she couldn't. There *was* a woman in his life, a woman he missed very much.

Her heart sank. What did she expect? She was twenty-eight, yet no one questioned her single status. He was only a few years older, yet the times he had lived in dictated early marriage. "Do you?" she asked gently. "Do you have a wife waiting for you?"

His jaw tightened and she saw a nerve twitch in his cheek. "No," he replied, his voice ragged. "I have no wife, no . . . family."

Meredith breathed a silent sigh of relief, but she quickly admonished herself. She would do well to remember that Griffin Rourke was not some fantasy pirate, but a flesh-and-blood man, a man with his own demons to plague his dreams. And he didn't belong here. If she continued to harbor these illusions about him, she'd only get hurt when he left.

If he left. The prospect of Griffin remaining in her time hung over them like a storm cloud. Whether she was attracted to him or not, it was her responsibility to see that he got home. She couldn't help believing that she had somehow brought him here, that he'd been an unwilling participant in some great cosmic happening.

"Why don't we go get some lunch," she suggested, hoping to shift the mood of their conversation. "I can work at the library later this afternoon."

"I am not hungry," he murmured. "I would like to take a walk. Alone."

Meredith nodded and pulled her hand from around his arm, knowing it would be best to leave him to his own thoughts. "I'll meet you back at the cottage then."

He nodded curtly, and without looking at her, set off down the street.

"Let him go," Meredith whispered to herself. "You'll have to let him go sooner or later, so do it now." As she watched him disappear around a bend in the road, she pressed her hand to her chest, wondering if her heart had heard the words she'd spoken.

THE NEXT TWO DAYS were passed in uneasy frustration, Griffin trying mightily to control his impatience and Meredith spending most of her time at the library, working at the computer. Griffin usually joined her, examining every scrap of information she uncovered, then demanding careful explanations.

But this morning, he had been in a foul temper, ready to give up on searching the computer networks. They'd argued over breakfast and she'd left him at the cottage to brood while she paced the pathways of cyberspace.

There was precious little to find that might help Griffin. What she did discover was purely theoretical, and often too difficult for her to understand. She was beginning to think that Griffin had been right, that this course of action would get them nowhere. She finally decided to head home and discuss her bleak findings with Griffin, to prepare him for the prospect that she might not be able to find him a way back.

She was secretly happy that she hadn't found anything. She wanted Griffin with her a little longer. At first, she'd rationalized that it was merely to benefit her work, but then she had to face the fact that she wanted more.

At night, she'd lie in bed and listen to him move about the cottage, hoping, praying, that he might come back to her bed as he had that first night. She would close her eyes and imagine his body next to hers, his breath soft on her neck, his lips nibbling a path—

Meredith stopped beside the road and cursed herself soundly. This would not do, these unbidden fantasies about Griffin Rourke! For all she knew, he might disappear just as quickly as he'd appeared, in a flash of lightning or a clap of thunder. She quickly put him out of her mind, replacing him with a mental grocery list before she took off in the direction of the store.

The sun was almost down by the time Meredith reached the cottage. In the waning light, she could make out a figure sitting on the steps. She breathed a silent sigh of relief, glad to see that Griffin was waiting for her. She shifted a bag of groceries in her arms and searched her jacket pocket for her keys.

"Hey there, Meredith!"

The figure on the steps stood up and waved. A flash of disappointment shot through her. This was not Griffin, but someone much shorter, with curly auburn hair. Slowly, Meredith smiled, recognizing her best friend, Dr. Kelsey Porterfield. "Kels!" she cried. "What are you doing here?"

"Do you have to ask? My graduate assistant told me you've called four times in the past three days. What is the big emergency?"

Meredith stepped up beside her and pushed the key into the lock. She opened the door and glanced around the interior, relieved to find that Griffin was not inside. She had plenty to explain to Kelsey without having to explain the presence of an eighteenth-century pirate living in her cottage. He was probably down at the harbor, watching the ferries come and go and the shrimpers return with their catch.

"You didn't have to drive all the way down here," she said, trying to sound nonchalant. "There's no emergency. I'm fine. I just had a few questions I needed to ask you."

Kelsey followed her into the cottage. "Come on, Meredith. You're the national poster child for patience. You didn't even bother to call me when you found out you were on the shortlist for the Sullivan Fellowship. I had to find out from that witch, Katherine Conrad, and her little band of campus cronies. You called four times!"

Meredith put the groceries down on the kitchen counter. "Did I? I'm sorry, but I didn't mean for you to rush down here."

"I was on my way back from my symposium at Wake Forest and decided to take a detour. I figured someone should check up on you, stuck here on this island with nothing but your books."

"I'm fine," Meredith repeated.

Kelsey studied her for a long moment, a shrewd look in her bright eyes. "You look all right, but whether you *are* all right is still to be determined. Why the frantic phone calls?"

"They weren't frantic," Meredith said. "I simply needed some information about . . . something . . . something you might know about. Would you like something to drink?"

Kelsey frowned, ignoring her question. "What is this mysterious something?"

Meredith sighed. "I—I was hoping you might be able to tell me about . . . about time travel." The last came out in a rush.

"Time travel?" Kelsey asked, her eyebrow arching in question.

"Yes, time travel. I—I've been thinking about writing a book, a novel, actually, and the whole premise of the book revolves around the possibility of time travel. So," she said, "is it?"

"Is it what?"

"Is it possible? Can someone travel in time?"

Kelsey grabbed the box of cereal from Meredith's hand and stuffed it back into the grocery bag. "Get your things," she ordered. "I'm taking you home. I don't know what's happened here, but I'm not letting you stay on this island an instant longer. You've got the Sullivan Fellowship riding on this next scholarly work of yours and you're thinking of writing a science fiction novel? The sooner you're back in an academic atmosphere, the better."

"I'm not crazy and I'm not leaving," Meredith said stubbornly. "Just tell me what I want to know. Please."

Kelsey looked into Meredith's eyes and sighed. "Only if you tell me what this is really about, because I know damn well it's not about writing a novel."

"I want to tell you," Meredith said, wincing, "but I'm not really sure *I* even know what it's about yet. I promise, I'll tell you as soon as I do."

An image of Griffin flashed in her mind and she felt a flood of desire wash over her. How she wanted to tell her best friend about the most incredible man she'd ever met— how blue his eyes were and how black his hair was. How she trembled when he touched her and how she dreamed of his kiss. But she couldn't.

Instead, she grabbed Kelsey's hand and pulled her over to the couch, then sat down beside her. "Explain what you know, in terms a history dweeb like me can understand."

Kelsey's expression was lined with concern and she shook her head in confusion.

"Please," Meredith begged, giving her friend's hand a squeeze.

Kelsey sighed, then tucked a curly strand of red hair behind her ear. "Well, theoretically, time travel is possible. In fact, all humans time-travel. We just do it at the same rate and in one direction—forward. But Einstein's theory of relativity opens the possibility that if we could travel faster than light, we could potentially travel into the future."

"So to jump into the future, a person would have to go really, really fast. Like on the Concorde."

Kelsey rolled her eyes. "Didn't you ever take a physics class in your pursuit of higher education? That's the speed of sound. The speed of light is 186,000 miles per second," she explained. "That's a whole lot faster than the Concorde."

"And what about going backward in time?" She sent up a silent prayer for Griffin, hoping that Kelsey's next words would prove to be the key to sending him back.

Kelsey shook her head. "It's not possible. There's no theoretical basis for it."

"But there has to be!" Meredith cried, jumping up from the couch. She paced the length of the room, gnawing on her thumbnail as she tried to accept Kelsey's pronouncement. "There just has to be."

"Well, there is the wormhole theory," Kelsey offered.

Meredith stopped and stared at her. "The what?"

"Wormhole. Black holes in space. If you go in one and come out the other side, you could travel in both time and space."

Meredith's spirits rose and she smiled in encouragement. "So let's say I went into one of these wormholes. Could I go back in time to the 1700s, and could I end up in, let's say... Bath, North Carolina?"

"I suppose," Kelsey replied. "But why would you want to go to Bath, North Carolina? Does this have something to do with your Blackbeard research?"

Meredith ignored her question, trying to logically sort through all the information she had been given, knowing how important it was to Griffin's future... and to hers. "So, could I have a wormhole in my backyard?"

"What is this all about?" Kelsey cried, jumping to her feet and throwing her arms up in frustration.

Meredith closed her eyes and let a vision of her pirate drift through her thoughts. "Just answer the question, Dr. Porterfield," she said, tipping her head back and sighing.

"Sure. You've probably got hundreds of wormholes in your backyard, maybe even thousands, but they all have worms living in them. As far as we know, wormholes only exist in space and that's only a theory, because no one's really ever seen one."

"I don't care if no one's ever seen a wormhole. Tell me about the theory."

"You really want me to explain? Meredith, you can't tell a gluon from a meson. And don't forget our little luncheon conversation about quarks a few months back. You said it gave you a migraine. How do you expect to understand wormholes?"

"I don't need to understand them completely. I just need to know if there could be a wormhole outside my back door."

Kelsey rubbed her forehead as if she'd suddenly developed a nagging headache of her own. "It's possible. I suppose we really can't rule it out."

"And going through a wormhole could send a person forward or back."

"The physics of the black-hole theory would support that."

Meredith drew in a deep breath and let it out in one big whoosh, then smiled. "I'm not crazy then. You don't know how much I needed to hear that."

Kelsey grabbed Meredith's hands and stared at her. "You've been working too hard, haven't you? Alone in this cottage for hours on end. Your mind is starting to . . . wander."

"That's not it," she said.

"Then what is it?" Kelsey cried. "What is going on in that head of yours?" She stared at Meredith long and hard. Slowly, realization seeped into her expression and she sucked in a sharp breath. "Don't tell me you've had a close encounter."

Meredith felt a flush creep up her cheeks. Was it that evident? Could Kelsey tell that she'd spent the night with a pirate in her bed. That he'd held her as if they were lovers and that she'd imagined they were. "A close encounter? You—you mean, like, with a man?"

"No, silly, with an alien."

This time, Meredith had cause to look at Kelsey as if *she* were going crazy. She shook her head and laughed. "Don't be silly, Kels. I can assure you, I haven't had a close encounter with any little green men."

"Well, that's a relief," she said. "You were starting to worry me." She gave Meredith a sideways glance. "Wait a minute. Are you saying you've had a close encounter with a *real* man?"

"No!" Meredith cried, knowing that if she answered any other way, Kelsey would launch into a full-scale interrogation. She decided it would be wise to steer the conversation back to physics. "So, let's say someone came through this wormhole and he wanted to go back. If you can't see these wormholes, how would one go about figuring out where they are?"

"Forget what I just said. I'm still worried. Is there a man behind all this?"

"Tell me how I find the wormholes!"

"I don't know," Kelsey said. "Maybe you just call a really big robin and tell it to go fetch itself a little snack."

"Very funny," Meredith said. "Now give me a straight answer."

"I'll admit, I *am* the most brilliant physicist I know, but there are some things that are beyond me."

"Hypothesize. That's what you physicists are good at, aren't you?"

Kelsey flopped back down on the couch and tipped her head back. She stared at the ceiling for a long time before she spoke. "Well, I suppose it would help to duplicate the conditions that were present when the original time-travel incident occurred. Go back to the same place, at the same time of the day. Maybe do the same things, wear the same clothes . . . ? I really don't know, Meredith. I'm just guessing."

"An educated guess is better than nothing," Meredith murmured. "I'll have to be satisfied with that much for now."

"So, are you planning a little trip back in time?" Kelsey teased. "Maybe you could dig up a few good sources and bring them back for posterity's sake? Just be careful, though," she warned.

"Of what?"

"Of changing the course of history," Kelsey said. "It could cause a lot of problems. Hey, while you're there, you can bring me back one of those romance-novel heroes, the guys in the tight britches and the lacy—" Kelsey stopped short, her eyes widening.

Meredith tried to contain the blush rising in her cheeks, but it was already too late. The hero she was describing sounded an awful lot like Griffin.

"I—I was joking," Kelsey stammered. "But—but you're not, are you?" Kelsey shivered then rubbed her arms. "Tell me what's going on here, Meredith. You're starting to scare me now."

Meredith grabbed Kelsey by the arm and pulled her up off the couch. "I'll tell you everything as soon as I have something to tell. Now, you have to go before you miss the last ferry to Hatteras."

"I was planning to stay overnight," Kelsey said, digging in her heels.

Meredith grabbed her friend's elbow and maneuvered her toward the door. "You can't. I have important things to do."

"No. I'm not leaving. If I have to, I'll get a hotel room. We *are* going to talk about all this. I am going to figure it out."

Meredith loosened her grip and groaned. "All right. You want the truth? There *is* a man and if you're here when he gets back, it will spoil all my plans for a night of hot sex. I want you to get into your car and take the next ferry out of here. And I promise, I will call you with all the pertinent details just as soon as I have them. Are you satisfied?"

Kelsey smiled smugly. "I knew it. I knew it all the time. You can't hide anything from me, Meredith. This is wonderful," she said, pulling open the door. "This is just what you need. So, is this man good in bed?"

Meredith gently pushed her out the door. "I don't know yet," she replied. Though she certainly hoped he might be around long enough for her to find out.

"Well, as soon as you do, you have to call and tell me. Promise you'll call?"

"I promise," Meredith said, leaning against the edge of the door. She paused, then reached out and hugged her friend. "Thanks for coming, Kels."

"No problem," Kelsey said with a grin. With that, she turned and headed toward her car, giving Meredith a little wave before she hopped inside and backed out onto the road.

Meredith closed the door and leaned against it, slowly letting out a tightly held breath. If Kelsey was right, then maybe there was a way to return Griffin to his own time. She had a good idea of how he'd gotten here in the first place. But the historian in her also wanted to know why.

Why had Griffin ended up here, in this time? Somehow, the notion that *she* had something to do with it was hard to deny. This whole affair wasn't just some cosmic mistake. After all, she was writing a book on Blackbeard and he knew the pirate personally. What more could she ask for in a research source? And then, there was her pirate fantasy.

But that couldn't be all there was to it. There had to be a more logical reason that fate had sent him here. Meredith pinched her eyes shut and searched her mind for an answer. If he wasn't here for her benefit, then maybe he had been sent for *his*. Was she supposed to help him in some way? Was there something she knew that he didn't? Or was she meant to prevent his participation in the events she had studied so closely?

Kelsey's warning about changing the course of history drifted through her mind. Exactly what did her friend mean by a lot of problems? And how could Meredith know whether her decisions would alter the past? She'd probably managed to lure a man right out of his century into hers, leaving a huge void where he'd once been. But then again, maybe sending him back would cause a problem.

Meredith groaned and rubbed her eyes with her fingertips. This was exactly why she was a historian instead of a scientist. She found no excitement in pondering a paradox like time travel. In fact, the whole subject was starting to give her a migraine.

GRIFFIN STARED UP at the garishly painted sign. The familiar image of a pirate in a tricorn and eye patch, with a dagger clutched between his teeth, looked down on him— the same picture he had on his underwear. Loud music, hypnotically rhythmic, pulsed through the screen door of the weathered waterfront building. A jumble of voices could be heard from the veranda behind the tavern as patrons leaned against a railing and stared out at the setting sun. The Pirate's Cove was a popular place, a place where he might be able to disappear into a crowd and enjoy a tankard or two.

Griffin pulled the screen door open and stepped inside. To his relief, only a few patrons noticed his arrival and they went back to their conversation after turning a brief glance in his direction. He spotted an empty stool in a dark corner at the end of the bar and headed toward it. His gaze was caught by row upon row of colorful glass bottles that lined the wall behind the bar and he cursed his naiveté.

Ordering a drink might be more complicated that he'd imagined. For all he knew, asking for an ale might mark him as an outsider and provoke questions he was not prepared to answer. Merrie would not appreciate that. She'd warned him what people might say if the truth were known. His voyage in time was not an everyday occurrence and if the townsfolk knew, they might think both of them had lost their minds.

Griffin couldn't fathom how this could be so, considering Merrie had told him he could wear a dress down Main Street without causing a stir. He smiled to himself. What would he have done without Merrie to help him navigate through the treacherous shoals of the twentieth century?

Over the past few days, he'd come to trust her, to depend on her for his very existence. If only there was a way to repay her for her kindness and understanding. But he possessed nothing more than the clothes she'd bought him and the pocketful of money she'd lent him. She deserved so much more.

His mind drifted to an image of her, standing beside him at the water's edge, the salt breeze blowing through her short-cropped hair. Like a needle on a compass, his thoughts always returned to her. She was his North Star, his lantern in the fog, and try as he might, he couldn't deny the attraction he felt toward her.

She was nothing like the women he had known in his life. Merrie possessed an inner strength, as if she knew exactly who she was and what she was about. And she was clever, maybe even in possession of a brilliant mind, if all those books she studied were any proof.

But it was not her mind that drove him to distraction. It was that body of hers, so soft and slender. He'd thought himself immune to those feelings, his heart hardened into stone by the losses in his life. But like a sculptor with a sharp chisel, Merrie had begun to chip away at his defenses with her gentle touch, her sweet kindness, stirring a desire he'd thought completely dead. To his surprise, his soul had responded with a buoyancy, a resiliency he thought he'd lost.

Griffin took a deep breath and slipped onto an empty stool at the bar. Most of the patrons had a small mug of amber-colored liquid that didn't resemble the nut-brown brew he was used to. And there was not a hogshead to be seen anywhere. The proprietor approached, a huge hulk of a man with a white apron tied around his considerable girth.

"What can I get you?" he asked, his voice gruff but friendly.

Griffin stared at the tavern keeper, suddenly unsure of what to say. "What might you have?" he countered smoothly.

The man slapped a folded handbill down on the bar and Griffin stared at it with relief. A long bill of fare was exactly what he needed to steer his way through this strange place. Yet he saw nothing familiar—no ale or posset or metheglin, not even a mention of cider. He scanned the list of strange names until the familiar words *rum* and *punch* caught his eye.

"I will have this," he said, pointing to the middle of the list.

The man's eyebrows shot up, but he didn't speak. "Anne Bonny's Grog? You sure you want that?"

Griffin nodded. He pulled out his money and placed it on the bar, but the man ignored it.

A few moments later, the tavern keeper returned with a strange concoction in an even stranger-looking glass. A tiny parasol and a plastic flower floated in the pink drink, the parasol skewering what Griffen assumed was fruit, though it didn't look like any fruit he'd ever seen. He took a hesitant swallow and smiled. Somewhere during the past few centuries, rum had mellowed from a hellish, eye-popping liquor to a smooth, subtle drink, barely perceptible beneath the exotic blend of fruit juice. He drained the glass and placed it on the bar.

"Another?" the tavern keeper asked.

Griffin nodded.

A second drink was placed in front of him. This time, Griffin sipped more slowly, savoring the sweet blend of juice and rum.

"You're Meredith's friend, aren't you?"

Griffin looked up. He'd known his presence on the island had caused some speculation, but he hadn't thought it would become talk for the taproom. Still, he shouldn't be surprised. He was blatantly living with an unmarried, and unchaperoned, woman. A woman with considerable charm, one that any man might find difficult to resist. "How have you come to know this?" Griffin asked.

The big man chuckled. "You're on an island, buddy. No such thing as privacy. Besides, Meredith's a born-and-bred Ocracoker. Her daddy was a shrimper on the island for years and her mama was the second cousin of our current police chief. We all watch out for our own, if you know what I mean." He sent Griffin a pointed look.

"I am her friend," Griffin said. "That much is so."

"Hmm. You two have a fight?"

"What?" Griffin asked. He'd never met a tavern keeper quite like this man. Idle gossip belonged in the the parlor with maiden aunts and in the kitchen with household servants, not at the local ordinary. But then, he and Merrie hadn't parted on the best of terms this morning. Damn, his temper. When would he learn to control it?

"We did not have a fight," Griffin replied grudgingly. "Just a few cross words at breakfast." He would make a point to apologize as soon as he returned to the cottage. And he would vow never to inflict his boorish moods on her again. "To be perfectly truthful, *I* had a few cross words. She merely listened."

"So you're in the doghouse," Tank stated, nodding his head in understanding.

"Doghouse?" Griffin asked.

"You know, banished to the sofa? No more nooky?"

"Nooky?" Griffin frowned, at a complete loss to understand the man's meaning.

"Hey, I'm a bartender," he said. "It's not that I'm nosy, but we're supposed to ask." He held out his hand. "Trevor Muldoon. My friends call me Tank."

Griffin shook his hand. "I am Rourke. Griffin Rourke. My friends call me Griff."

"You don't sound like you're from around here, Griff," Tank said. He picked up a wet glass from beneath the bar and dried it distractedly. "What is that accent—British? You from England?"

Griffin scrambled for an answer. "Yes," he replied, certain that was safe enough. "London." He shifted on the stool. All he'd wanted was a drink and now he was stuck with an inquisition that rivaled the Spanish. If he was lucky, Tank's knowledge of England would be limited and the questions would stop here and now.

"You're a long way from home," Tank commented. "How long do you plan to stay round these parts?"

The real inquiry was subtly hidden beneath Tank's innocent question. *How long do you intend to reside with Meredith?* Griffin shrugged. "I haven't decided," he replied.

"You and Meredith an item?" Tank asked, his gaze moving from his task to watch Griffin.

"An item?"

"A thing," he clarified. "Are you . . . together?"

"I—I am not sure of your meaning," Griffin said. Was he asking him if he and Merrie slept in the same bed? Or was he questioning what went on in that bed?

Tank snorted. "When it comes to women, no one's ever sure, right, Griff?"

Griffin forced a smile. His relationship with Merrie was not a fit subject for public discussion and he wasn't about to let this go any further. Besides, at this moment, he wasn't sure exactly what his relationship with the fair Merrie was.

"So," Tank said, "have you and Merrie been keepin' company for a long time?"

"Not long," Griffin said. He drew a long breath. "I have been wondering what a man does around here to make a wage." The change in topic was clumsy, but the tavern keeper didn't seem to notice.

"You mean, like a job?" Tank asked.

Griffin nodded, not wanting to say the words, but compelled to ask. Over the past few days, he'd been considering what the future might hold. Merrie had found nothing in her little computer box to help him, and her friend still hadn't called. He couldn't just sit still and wait for something to happen. He needed to occupy himself, or risk losing his mind. And he couldn't continue to live off Merrie's charity.

"If I would decide to stay on this island," Griffin said, "I will need to find work."

Tank grunted and shook his head. "Jobs are hard to come by on Ocracoke. Either you make a living off the tourists or you make your money on the water. Beyond that, there's not much left. What kind of work do you do?"

"I have made my living on the sea, crossing the Atlantic on a merchant ship."

"Well, I can watch out for something on one of the fishing boats," Tank said. "Can't promise much, though."

"I would appreciate that," Griffin said. "Thank you."

A man at the other end of the bar called Tank's name, and to Griffin's relief, the tavern keeper turned and walked away. Griffin sat alone for a long time, listening to the strange music that filled the room and watching the other patrons while he had more of Anne Bonny's Grog. This was what he was hoping for—a dark corner, a numbing drink and a moment to consider what lay ahead.

He'd spent the last few days at war with himself, refusing to believe that he might never get back. But he was a practical man, a man who was used to thinking on his feet and attacking a problem head-on. If he couldn't return, he'd have to find a position that paid a wage and make a new life for himself. He was not a man who would consider being kept by a woman, even a woman as kind and compassionate as Merrie.

Griffin cursed himself and downed the rest of his rum punch in one long gulp. What was wrong with his head? Was the course he'd set against Teach so meaningless that he'd given it up already? Merrie or no Merrie, he could not stay here—he would not. He didn't belong here, he belonged in his own time. Teach was waiting.

Griffin grabbed the remainder of his money and shoved it in his pocket, then slid off the stool, ready to take his leave. But Tank approached, another drink in his hand. He placed it in front of Griffin and grinned.

"I did not call for another drink," Griffin said.

"This one's compliments of the lady over there." Tank cocked his head in the direction of a young woman sitting on the far corner of the bar. She crooked her little finger at him and tossed her red hair over her shoulder. He had seen that coy smile on more than one willing tavern wench.

There was a time, after Jane's death, that he would have strolled drunkenly over to her and pulled her lush body against his. She'd smell of other men, but he wouldn't care. He'd slip a coin between her breasts and they'd climb the stairs to a well-used room where he'd lift her skirts and slake his need.

Griffin grabbed the glass and tipped it in the woman's direction, then drained it. She slowly slipped off her stool and sauntered toward him. He waited until she stood at his side, her ample breasts pressed against his upper arm, her perfume thick in the air.

"Hi," she cooed. "You're new around here, aren't you?"

He looked down into her inviting gaze, then at her pouting red-painted lips. Ripe and ready to be plucked. It didn't matter which century he was in, he knew what she wanted. And what he should want, as well.

But instead, he found himself comparing this woman to his sweet Merrie. Merrie who smelled of fresh air and soap. Merrie who needed no paint to enhance her pretty features and whose slender, almost boyish body had curled against him in sleep. Merrie who asked nothing of him, but gave him so much.

Griffin reached into his pocket and pulled out what was left of his money. He pressed the wad of bills into the woman's hand. "I thank you for the drink," he said, "and the tempting offer. But I fear I cannot stay. I am in the . . ." He frowned, groping for the word. "Doghouse," he finally said. "I am in the doghouse and must find my way out before morning."

With that, he turned toward the door, leaving the woman gaping with shock and staring after him. No, he couldn't stay and enjoy what she offered. Merrie was waiting for him at home, and whether he wanted to admit it or not, he found more pleasure in the prospect of spending the wee hours of the night standing over Merrie's bed and watching her sleep, than he would losing himself in a stranger's body.

4

GRIFFIN BANGED his shin on a small table as he stumbled through the living room in the dark. He cursed softly, trying to remember how it was the lamps turned on and off, then paused for a moment and let his eyes adjust. A sliver of light shone from beneath Merrie's bedroom door.

He knocked softly and when she called out, he opened the door. Merrie looked up at him from her bed, her spectacles perched on the end of her nose. She held the little box that she called a laptop computer, and papers were scattered about her on the coverlet.

She looked so fresh-faced and lovely that desire welled up inside him and he had to fight the impulse to cross the room and pull her into his arms. Lord, he needed a woman right now, and he wanted that woman to be Merrie.

Fighting back his impulses, he forced a smile, an expression that she hesitantly returned. "I am glad to see I am not in the doghouse anymore," he said, strolling into the room to sit on the edge of the bed.

"The doghouse?" she asked.

"You are not angry with me."

"Why would I be angry?" she asked.

He frowned. "In my century, a woman does not like a man to stay out late at night, drinking ale and telling tales with his friends."

"Is that what you were doing?" She sniffed, then crinkled her nose. "Which one of them was wearing the cheap perfume?" she asked dryly.

He ignored her last question in favor of the first. "Not ale. Rum." He reached inside his shirt pocket and pulled out a handful of tiny parasols and plastic flowers. "And a fine drink it was. I brought these for you." He pushed a parasol up and down, still amazed at how they worked. "I don't understand why they are used to hold fruit, but I found them interesting."

Merrie picked up one of the parasols and played with it, smiling. He found his attention captured by her mouth...her soft, moist lips that cried out to be kissed...kissed by him...long and hard.

"Thank you," she said. "That was very thoughtful." She counted the umbrellas. "You drank six of Tank's rum punches?"

He blinked and turned his gaze away from the intimate study of her mouth. "They tasted good and he kept placing them in front of me. It would have been rude to refuse."

Merrie sighed and looked at him with large, green eyes. "I'm sorry that you're so unhappy here," she said softly. "I wish I could help you, but I don't know how. I'm trying my best."

He was struck again by how beautiful she looked. He reached out to smooth the lines of worry from her forehead and a rush of warmth traveled though him, pooling at his core, as he touched her silken skin. "I have a bad temper, that is true, but I don't mean to abuse you with it." Griffin slowly moved his thumb across her lower lip, resisting the temptation to cover her mouth with his. "I am sorry for my harsh words. And I am thankful for what you have done for me, Merrie-girl."

"But you want to go home," she said, her eyes wide.

He sighed and picked up her hand, then wove his fingers through hers, wondering at how tiny and delicate she was. "I have no choice," he said, forcing himself to believe the words. "I must."

She drew a deep breath and he felt her fingers tighten around his. "My friend, Kelsey, stopped by while you were out. She was on her way back to Williamsburg from her symposium."

Griffin snapped his head up, his heart stopping in his chest. "What did she say?"

"The only advice she could offer for now was that we should try to duplicate the conditions of that night. Then maybe we can find the hole in time that you stepped through."

Griffin bit back a curse. "Duplicate a hurricane? Unless you have found a way to change the weather in this century, that sounds nearly impossible."

"Maybe we don't actually need a hurricane," Merrie explained. "Hopefully, any storm will do. Maybe even a good hard rain."

"So we just have to wait for a storm?"

"For now. Until we figure out another way."

Griffin pulled in the reins on his temper. She didn't deserve another of his angry outbursts. He had put her through too much already. "You told your friend, Kelsey, about me?" he asked evenly.

She shook her head. "I just gave her a hypothetical situation. I told her I was thinking of writing a novel. If I'd told her the truth, she would have put me on the first bus to the funny farm."

Griffin opened his mouth to ask just what a "bus" and a "funny farm" were, then realized he was still in the dark about "nooky." He ignored the impulse to investigate further. Instead, he pushed himself off the bed and began to pace the room. He felt her eyes following him. "What time of day did you find me?" he asked.

"Midnight," she replied.

"And what were the conditions?"

"Very weird," she recalled. "The storm was raging outside, and then all of a sudden, it stopped. It became so calm it was frightening."

"And how did you find me?"

She frowned. "I'm not sure, but I remember feeling compelled to go outside. I was just looking around and there you were."

"Where?"

"In the backyard."

He stepped to the bedroom window and pulled back the lace curtain. "Where, precisely?"

"About five yards straight out from the big cedar," she replied. "The water was really high. The waves were almost halfway across the lawn."

Griffin stared out into the dark and considered all she had told him, trying to remember something, anything, about that night. But from the time he'd fallen overboard and hit the water until the time he'd woken up on her sofa, his mind was a blank.

"There is one other thing," Merrie said softly.

"What is that?"

"I—I was thinking that maybe my beach isn't the place this started. Maybe it's just where you ended up."

"I don't understand," Griffin said.

"I called a charter service after I spoke with Kelsey and I've rented a sailboat for a few days. If the weather is good, we can leave tomorrow. I thought we could sail across the Sound, up the Pamlico River and find the spot where you fell in. We might find a clue. It's a long day's sail, so we can moor the boat in Bath and spend the night there, then sail back the next day."

"That is a clever plan, Merrie-girl," he said, turning to her in surprise. "Do you know how to sail?"

"My father and I used to have a little boat when I was a child. And what I don't remember, you can fill in. I don't think sailing has changed that much over the past three hundred years."

For the first time since he'd arrived in this place, he felt a sense of hope. If he could get back within a week, he might be able to salvage his plan to bring Blackbeard down. He would be glad to leave, for there was nothing of interest to him here . . . except Merrie.

Over the past few days, he'd been surprised at the depth of her spirit and resolve. Though he'd been in a foul mood, she hadn't backed down from him. She didn't run to her bedchamber, weeping at his surly treatment. Nor did she pout for days on end, or send for her mother and her sisters. Instead, she constantly challenged him, forcing him to see this place for what it had to offer.

She was a strong woman, a woman that a man could depend on. And he couldn't deny his feelings for her any longer. He cared about her and her happiness, and he didn't feel at all comfortable about leaving her here alone. But he had a task that he must complete and nothing must stand in his way.

He slowly let the curtain drop and returned to sit on the bed, his back to her. He scrubbed at his eyes with the heels of his hands, then raked his fingers through his hair. "What if I can't get back?" he murmured.

He felt her hand on his shoulder, warm and reassuring, and he closed his eyes, giving in to her gentle touch.

"We'll think about that if and when the time comes," she said.

Griffin turned and looked into Merrie's eyes. As long as he was determined to return, she would support his choice, of that he was certain. His gaze dropped to her mouth again, her lips so lush and ripe. "Why are you alone?" he asked.

She blinked, confusion clouding her expression. "I—I don't understand."

"Why is there no man to protect you? When I leave, you'll have no one. Are you not afraid?"

A winsome smile curved the corners of her mouth. "I don't need someone to protect me, Griffin," she said. "I'm all right on my own."

"But you are well past the age of marriage, and—"

"And where you come from they'd call me a spinster or an old maid, right?"

"A thornback," he added.

"Well, I wouldn't care what they called me."

"Then you prefer to live this way. Alone?"

Her cheeks took on a pink glow and she shrugged. "I don't know. I guess I don't think about it, Griffin. It's not that important to me. The sexual revolution gave me, and all women, choices. I have my career and if I want, I can have a husband, also."

He was going to ask what the sexual revolution was, but decided to return to more pressing matters. "Well, I believe it is important. You must choose a husband. You must not put it off any longer."

"It's not as easy as that," Merrie said. "There are many things to consider."

"What about this Muldoon? He seems like a good man, he is even-tempered and healthy, he owns a large establishment with many patrons. He would make you a fine husband. I could approach this man with an offer if you would like."

"Tank Muldoon and me?" Merrie considered the match for only a moment before she laughed, a warm musical sound that filled the room. "Tank is a very nice man, but he's not my type."

He pressed her hands between his. "He is strong and honest and wealthy and his appearance is not in the least objectionable. I know it is important to a woman to have a man that bathes regularly and has good teeth."

"Let me put it another way. I'm not Tank's type."

"He would be a lucky man to have you."

As would I, Griffin thought. But it could not be, for he and Merrie had been doomed from the start. They came from different lives and places, sharing only this short moment in time before all would be set right.

She pulled her hands from his and idly fussed with the bed linens, tucking them snugly around her. "Griffin, don't worry about me. I'll be fine after you leave. I was fine before you came, wasn't I?"

He nodded then cupped her cheek in his palm, tipping her gaze up to his. "If I lived in your time, I would offer for you."

She covered his fingers with her own. "That would be very noble of you. But I wouldn't want you to offer for me, unless you loved me."

"Many marry without love," he said. He hadn't loved Jane when he'd offered for her. In fact, he had barely known her. Yet over the two years they had been married, they had grown to care for each other. And when he'd lost her, he felt as if his heart had been torn from his body and buried beside her and their baby. Maybe he had loved her, but then, he would never truly be sure.

She had died alone, in their small house in Williamsburg, three days after the fever had taken his infant son—the son he'd never seen or held. And where had he been, but on his way home from London, busy with his duties as captain of the *Spirit* and gloating over the fine price he had secured for his cargo of Virginia tobacco.

"Griffin?"

He blinked and found her staring at him.

"Are you all right?" she asked.

Slowly, without speaking, he bent forward and touched his mouth to hers. She didn't pull away or play the coy maiden. Instead, Merrie returned his kiss, parting her lips slightly, inviting him to take more. And when he didn't, she did, touching her tongue to his lower lip, gently tempting, teasing.

What began as a simple gesture of thanks, suddenly vibrated with an overwhelming sensuality. He wanted to feel her mouth beneath his, bury his face in her sweet-smelling hair, then gaze into her passion-clouded eyes.

It took all his strength to draw away. He could not take what she offered, not in this time, not in any time. He had no right, for he could not offer her anything in return. Dropping his hand from her soft cheek, he sucked in a deep draft of air, averting his gaze from the apprehension that colored her deep green eyes.

"I—I'm sorry," she said.

"There is no need to apologize," Griffin replied. "I am the one to be sorry. I acted impulsively, without thought for your feelings, or your honor."

He quickly stood and walked to the bedroom door.

"You don't have to leave," she said.

"I do," he replied. "'Tis nearly midnight. Your friend said that we must try to duplicate what happened. Perhaps it wasn't the weather, but the time or the place. I'm of a mind to wait outside and see."

Merrie sat up straight in bed. "Do you think it will work?"

Griffin shrugged. "We'll not know until we try." He smiled. "Go to sleep, Merrie-girl," he said softly. "And if I am gone when you wake, you will think this has all been a dream."

"I'll never believe it was a dream," she said, her voice trembling slightly. "I'll never forget you."

"Nor I you," he said.

Griffin turned and walked out of the bedroom, leaving Merrie alone. She would be fine, she had assured him of that fact. Merrie had lived alone for a long time before he had come to her. Still, in a small corner of his soul, he knew he was leaving something rare and precious behind. And if he magically stepped back to his own time on this night, he knew he would always wonder what might have been had he been forced to stay.

He had spoken the truth when he said he would not forget her. He would see her eyes in the sea and her smile in the sun. He would feel her skin when he touched the finest silk and he would smell her perfume every time he brought a flower to his nose.

No, upon his life, he would never forget Merrie.

MEREDITH FLOPPED BACK on her pillow and covered her face with her hands. She felt like crying but she wasn't sure why. This man had blown into her life with all the force of a hurricane, and now there was a good chance he'd blow right back out again.

She knew she had to let him go. There was nothing for him here, and he was intent on his plan to avenge his father's death. And yet, she didn't want him to leave. There was something about him, something she felt on such a visceral level, a feeling that she couldn't put into words, something that told her this thing between them was not finished. He was not supposed to leave, not yet.

Meredith fought against the temptation to run out to the beach and try to convince him to stay. But deep down, she knew that would be wrong. She had to let him try, and if nothing happened this night, she would put her feelings aside and continue to help him until he found his way back.

With a groan of frustration, Meredith climbed out of bed and walked to the window. Drawing a deep breath, she pulled back the curtain and looked out into the yard. He stood on the lawn, his form illuminated by the full moon, his hair blowing in the breeze.

He stared out at the water, watching, waiting. A halo of silver light seemed to surround him, gilding his body like some ancient statue of a sea god, lining a shimmering path from his feet out to the horizon. He looked so far away, already lost to her, and she touched her lips with her fingers, hoping to feel the warmth of his mouth still there. But her lips were cold, his touch long gone.

Meredith glanced over at the bedside clock. Her stomach tightened as the numbers changed to 11:57. She let the lace curtain fall from her fingers and numbly walked back to the bed. Shoving all her papers to the floor, she crawled beneath the covers and curled into a tiny ball.

She was frightened, not of what she had been through, but of what the future might be without him. Would she ever feel this powerful attraction for a man again? Or would she be left with her memories of Griffin and her half-finished dreams?

Reaching over, she turned off the bedside lamp and let the darkness envelop her. As she closed her eyes, an image of him flashed in her mind, imprinted on her memory. "Go to sleep," she whispered, rolling over on her back to stare at the ceiling. "What will happen, will happen. If he isn't meant to leave, he won't."

She lay perfectly still for a very long time, listening to the sounds around her and inside her: the waves, her heartbeat, the breeze, her breathing and the silent cry of an abandoned soul. The clock marked each minute and as it did, she was forced to face the fact that he was gone. He'd disappeared from her life as quickly as he'd appeared. She squeezed her eyes shut and tried to sleep.

Meredith wasn't sure how much time had passed—she'd been afraid to open her eyes and look at the clock. Maybe she'd even drifted off for a few minutes. But slowly, she realized that she wasn't alone anymore. He was here, in the room. She sensed his presence as surely as if the light was on and she was staring at his handsome face.

She heard him approach the bed and for a moment he stood over her, his breathing deep and even. Then she heard him whisper her name. Her heart leaped and she fought the urge to jump up and throw her arms around him in joy. Instead, she keep her eyes closed and her body still.

The bed sank beneath his weight. He moaned softly as he pulled her against him, pressing her backside into his lap and wrapping his arms around her waist. She knew he just needed to be with someone, anyone, right now, but she was thankful he'd chosen her. For the first time, she understood the loneliness he felt, isolated and so far from everything familiar. She'd felt that same loneliness as she watched him on the beach.

Still, though she knew he was in pain, a lazy sense of comfort and satisfaction worked its way through her body. She felt exhausted, yet strangely exhilarated. He was here with her, where he belonged, at least for a little while longer.

When she was certain he slept, Meredith slipped out of his arms and turned on the bedside lamp. The light spilled across his face and she held her breath, waiting for him to open his eyes. But he was deep in slumber, his perfect features tranquil and untroubled.

She turned on her side and faced him, lazily studying every detail of his face. Dark lashes, sinfully long for a man, and flawlessly arched eyebrows, as black as raven's wings, framed his eyes. Taken alone, they would have appeared almost feminine, but amidst the strong cheekbones, the sculpted mouth and the aristocratic nose, they fell into a remarkable masculine balance.

He had changed back into his old clothes before going out to the beach, but he had discarded his waistcoat before crawling into bed with her. His linen shirt gaped open in the front, revealing a wide expanse of smooth chest, dusted with dark hair. She reached out and held her hand close to his skin, close enough to feel the warmth radiating into her fingers, yet not close enough to touch him. Slowly, she skimmed her fingers above the ridges of his muscles, imagining the feel of him, without making contact.

As she explored his body this way, first with her eyes and then with an invisible touch, she marveled at the man who shared her bed . . . the man who had kissed her earlier . . . the man who had awakened feelings she never knew she possessed.

She'd had a number of relationships with colleagues on campus, always more intellectual than anything else. But she'd never felt for them what she felt for Griffin. Though she had tried to convince herself she was sexually attracted to these men, when it came right down to consummating the relationship, she couldn't bring herself to go through with it.

In this day and age, her virginity loomed over her like a big scarlet *V*, a quality that most men felt was more odd than admirable. So maybe she was a little repressed, but all repression aside, she couldn't deny her attraction to Griffin.

He was the opposite of everything she'd thought she wanted in a man—he was a man of action, not introspection. He could be brooding and distant, keeping his emotions locked deep inside. Griffin Rourke was definitely not a sensitive, nineties kind of guy. But she didn't want that. She wanted him—exactly the way he was, with all his simmering arrogance and sensual energy and chauvinistic ideas.

Maybe that was why she felt so at ease around him. In the past, just the thought of making love to a man had caused her paroxysms of nervousness. But Griffin knew nothing about the games that men and women played in today's society. To him, she appeared sophisticated and self-assured, a woman of action, and in his presence, she'd begun to believe as much of herself.

She groaned inwardly. If only that were true. If only she *were* a woman of action, she might be able to touch him, instead of just holding her hand so near to his body. Or she might have the nerve to kiss him, instead of just staring at his lips. Or she might even make love to him, instead of fantasizing about it.

She watched him for a long time, inhaling the scent of him, committing every detail of Griffin Rourke to her mind, knowing that at any moment, he might be snatched from her life forever.

As her eyes finally drifted shut and she felt herself slipping toward sleep, she knew that it didn't matter how much time they had left. It would never be enough. And yet, it had to be. For whatever it was—a day, a week, a year—it would have to last her a lifetime.

RAIN DRUMMED GENTLY on the roof of the cottage. Griffin stood at the window and stared out at the steel gray sky and the dark water below. The trees in the yard swayed against a fine breeze which blew across the Sound to the mainland. Thunder rumbled in the distance, low and deep. With a silent oath, he turned and looked at Merrie. She sat on the sofa, her legs curled beneath her, books spread all about her, perfectly happy to stay inside.

"I have sailed in weather much worse than this," he said. "The wind is perfect for a quick sail up the Pamticoe."

"Pamlico," Merrie corrected distractedly. "And I'm sure you have."

"You would not be in any danger."

She looked up at him with doubtful green eyes. "There is nothing that you can say that will get me out on the water today, so you might as well relax."

"Relax," Griffin muttered. "I cannot relax. I don't understand this preoccupation you have with relaxing. We have been relaxing for three days, waiting for this weather to clear. 'Tis only rain."

After three nights waiting on the beach, waiting for time to swallow him up again, he was anxious to try something new. Their trip to Bath had given him new hope. A visit to where it all began might provide answers to the way back.

"We're in the middle of hurricane season. I'm not going out on the water until the sky is perfectly clear and that's that." She glanced up at him. "Can't you find something better to do than pace the room and curse beneath your breath? Why don't you take a walk?"

"I do not find aimless walking about a relaxing venture," he replied.

"What do you colonials do for fun? You must have something to occupy your leisure time."

"There is fox hunting and cockfighting," Griffin said.

"I meant like a hobby," Meredith said.

"Horse racing, wrestling matches. Sometimes there are parties with dancing and gambling . . . and drinking, of course."

Meredith frowned. "All right, maybe there isn't much of interest to occupy your time here. We'll just have to find you some new hobbies."

"To what end? What would this pointless activity accomplish? Would it turn me a better profit or make my life easier?"

Merrie blinked, then frowned, a look of consternation crossing her pretty features. "No," she finally said. "But it would give me time to do my own work."

Griffin sighed inwardly at her edgy reply. Would he ever learn to control his impatience? It was his least admirable quality, right behind his stubborn nature. "All right," he relented. "I would agree that during my time here, I could make use of a hobby."

Her smile was worth his capitulation, for it warmed him to the very center of his soul.

"Good," Merrie said. "Now, what did you usually do on a rainy day back in your time?"

He grinned lasciviously. "I can think of only one thing," he teased. "And I would guess things have not changed that much in this century."

"I'm talking about hobbies, here," Merrie said, understanding his meaning immediately. "What would you like to be doing . . . for fun . . . I mean, for a hobby?"

Griffin considered the question for a long minute then shook his head. Besides spending a rainy afternoon in bed with a warm and willing woman, the only other thing he could imagine doing was standing on the deck of his own ship, feeling the swell of the sea beneath his feet and the rain on his face, hearing the snap of the sails above his head. He'd been born to captain a ship, to realize the dreams his father had of building a vast shipping empire on the profits from tobacco.

From the time Griffin was a boy, his father had talked as if Griffin's destiny had already been determined. He was an only child, and he and his father had been inseparable, and of one mind. By the time he was ten, he knew every facet of growing tobacco. And he also knew that every crop of tobacco harvested on the Rourke plantation was crucial to realizing the dream.

Finally, after years of planning, the ship was built, and the empire founded. They christened their first ship the *Betty*, after his mother, and launched the sloop on Griffin's twelfth birthday. And from that day onward, Griffin's life was promised to the sea.

He could still recall with such clarity the look of pride on his father's face as the boat slipped into the water. The *Betty* was his father's life, the business of the ship sustaining him after Griffin's mother died.

And then Teach took it all away. The pirate attacked and captured the *Betty* off the Virginia shore while his father was on board. The brigands stole what cargo they fancied, then scuttled the ship with the rest still in the hold.

"What is the date?" he asked softly, stopping to stare at a strangely silent Ben Gunn.

"September twenty-sixth," Merrie replied.

He stroked the parrot's breast with his finger. "Nearly a year gone by," Griffin murmured. "That is when this tangle began."

"What tangle?"

"Teach and me…and my father." His voice was flat and emotionless. He barely recognized it as his own.

"Can you tell me what happened?" Merrie asked.

Griffin turned away from the parrot and began to pace again, stopping at the window to check the weather once more. "Teach killed him," he finally said. "There is nothing more to tell."

"That's strange," Merrie said.

He turned and stared at her. "And why is that?"

"Even though Blackbeard fashioned a wicked image for himself, he didn't go down in history as a bloodthirsty murderer. We know that sailors on merchant ships were superstitious and they believed him to be the devil himself. But the sources say he managed to capture most of his booty without a fight."

Griffin felt his temper rise. How could she defend such a man? Had the pirate Blackbeard merely become some romantic myth, a colorful hero whose evil deeds had faded with the passage of time? "He murdered my father," Griffin repeated, trying to keep his voice even, "as surely as if he had run him through with his own cutlass."

Merrie drew a deep breath. "I'm sorry. Would you like to talk about it?"

"No," Griffin said. "There is nothing more to be said."

"But maybe if you talked about it, you might—"

"No," he repeated. "Talking will not bring back my father, so what is the point to it?"

"All right," Merrie snapped. "We won't talk." She pointed to the place on the floor at her feet. "Sit!" she ordered. "And relax!"

He glared at her through narrowed eyes, then grudgingly did as he was told. She handed him a boating magazine.

"You're making *me* tense," she said.

He sat on the floor for a moment then sighed and tossed the magazine on the low table in front of him. "You see, I cannot relax. It is not part of my nature."

Merrie placed her hands on his shoulders and pushed him back down. With a frustrated oath, she settled behind him on the couch, pulling him against the cushions, her legs on either side of his shoulders, her bare feet braced along his thighs.

She placed her hands on his shoulders and slowly began to knead the muscles on either side of his neck. Her fingers were strong and warm and he closed his eyes, letting a tightly held breath escape his chest. He'd never been touched by a woman in this manner, but he found the casual contact wonderfully enjoyable.

"You truly are the most impatient man I've ever met," Merrie said.

Griffin smiled. "I inherited that quality from my father. He was never satisfied with tomorrow, or even today. Everything had to be done yesterday. My mother would become so angry with him that she would not speak to him until he would agree to take her for a long carriage ride."

"She sounds like a sensible woman."

"She was." He tipped his head back and sighed contentedly. "My father once owned her and she proved to be so sensible, he had to marry her."

"He owned her?" Merrie asked.

"My father came to the colonies in 1670 when he was twenty years old, straight away from the gallows where he'd been sent for petty theft. And when he arrived, his articles of indenture were auctioned off to the highest bidder. He worked on a tobacco plantation for fifteen years before he was free to start a life of his own."

Merrie's fingers stilled for a moment. "That must have been very difficult for him."

"Don't stop," Griffin murmured.

"What?"

"This thing you are doing with your fingers. Don't stop," he repeated.

Merrie continued to work magic with her fingers, lulling him into a lazy state of languor. He felt like a cat, stretched out in a spot of sunshine, completely content with his lot in life.

"Tell me more," she said.

"By the time he was free, he had learned two things," Griffin continued. "The first was how to raise tobacco and make a profit at it. The second was a deep and abiding hatred of slavery. Instead of owning slaves, he would buy only the articles of redemptioners, those who came to the colonies of their own free will, and after four years of work, he would give them new clothing, a gun and enough money to buy fifty acres of land."

"In 1665, former indentured servants constituted almost half of the membership of Virginia's House of Burgesses," Merrie said.

Griffin twisted around and looked at her in surprise. "I did not know that."

She smiled winsomely and shrugged. "I'm a history professor. I've mentioned that fact in my lectures for years, but it never really meant anything until now. Go on with your story."

"There's not much more to tell. My mother was an orphan from Bristol. As soon as she was of an age, she came to the colonies. My father saw her on the docks that day and fell in love with her, then and there. He bought her papers and she tended his house for five months before he finally convinced her to marry him."

Merrie wrapped her arms around his neck and rested her chin on the top of his head. "That's such a wonderful story," she said. "So romantic."

Griffin smoothed his palms along her arms, enjoying the warmth of her pleasant embrace. How easy it was between them, this gentle friendship that they shared. She seemed to know how to make him happy, how to turn his foul moods fair. He'd never been friends with a woman, especially with a woman he desired.

He had always considered women weaker, less able to handle the stresses of daily life and the concerns of a man's world. But Merrie was equal to a man in every way, strong and determined, independent and stubborn. He felt as if he could talk to her about anything, confide in her about his fears and his doubts, his hopes and his dreams.

"As soon as my father had enough money saved, he sold the plantation," Griffin continued, "and had his first ship built. I remember the day he took me on board. I was twelve years old. He named her the *Betty,* after my mother, Elizabeth, and he began to sail the coast and the rivers, taking British goods south and bringing tobacco and furs and indigo north to Norfolk for shipment to England. When I turned twenty-one, he gave me a ship of my own and I sailed the route from Norfolk to London."

"That's pretty young for such a responsibility," Merrie said. "At twenty-one, most of my undergraduate male students are more concerned with girls and partying. You were barely a man and you were sailing the ocean."

"I was captain of my own ship," Griffin said. "And I had already crossed the Atlantic more times than many men in my crew. My father put me on board a friend's ship as a cabin boy when I turned thirteen and I worked my way through the ranks. When I was seventeen, I took a year away from the sea for an education. And at eighteen, I served as a lieutenant on a brigantine that sailed between the James River and the Thames."

She slipped her hands beneath the collar of his shirt and brushed her fingers softly along his nape. "You are a very brave man," she said, a tremble audible in her voice.

Merrie's fingers began to work again, but this time, with her touch firm against his bare skin, the contact seemed more intimate. He sank back and closed his eyes. A numbing warmth seeped through his tight muscles, slowly drifting down his torso and awakening a gentle throb of desire at his core. "I am not so brave," he murmured. "But there have been times of late when I wished I was."

"You must be anxious to finish this thing with Teach, so you can get back to your life," she said, her hesitant words clouded with hidden emotion.

Griffin paused before he spoke. He was eager to exact his revenge against the pirate, that much was true. But he hadn't really thought about his life beyond that. Now, as he did, he realized that the future seemed empty, void of the people he loved. His mother had died when he was fourteen. Later, he'd lost Jane and his son. And with his father now gone, he had no one left.

Griffin slowly turned to face her, kneeling between her legs. He grabbed her hands and pressed her fingers between his palms, staring deeply into her wide green eyes. "I cannot stay," he said. "If I could, I would. You must believe this is true."

"I—I wasn't asking you to stay," she said, her gentle voice uncertain.

"You have done so much for me," he said. "I feel that I owe you a great debt."

She tugged her fingers from his grasp. "No, you owe me nothing." Her words were edgy, defensive, as if he'd somehow insulted her.

Griffin placed his hand on her cheek. "You saved my life," he murmured. "And for that I will always be thankful." Her soft skin warmed his hand and heated his blood. She closed her eyes and turned into his touch. Lord, he couldn't help wondering what might come of them if he stayed.

She'd kindled something in him that he'd thought was long dead—buried with Jane—a growing need to share his life with a woman, an undeniable desire to make her his own. "I do owe you more than you will ever know, Merrie-girl."

Griffin bent nearer to her and brushed his lips across hers, relishing the silken touch of her mouth, a caress as soft as the petals of a rose. But he could not stop there, for what began as a simple gesture of gratitude flared into a passion so intense it made his pulse race.

He brought his lips down on hers again, this time demanding a response from her, pressing her back into the couch. A tiny moan escaped her throat and she opened to him and twisted her arms around his neck. He savored the sweet nectar of her mouth, a taste as heady as the finest Madeira, as addictive as Chinese opium. He wanted to stop, yet he couldn't draw away.

He'd never felt such a strong attraction to a woman, an attraction that seemed to overwhelm all common sense and reduce his every thought to the need for physical satisfaction. She used her experience well, drawing him in, making him want her all the more.

In such a short time, Merrie had become his safe harbor, a serene place where he could escape the terrible storms that had racked his existence on this earth. How he wanted to stay here, safe from the wind and the high waves, anchored in the lee of her comforting embrace, lost in the feel of her body beneath him, around him, beside him.

She had offered her body to him by her every wanton action, yet he couldn't help thinking of the other men in her life. Yes, he wanted her, but he wanted his revenge against the pirate even more. And to let her believe otherwise was the mark of a scoundrel, the trait of a blackguard who cared for no one but himself. He would not hurt her as she'd been hurt by men before. Steeling his resolve, he pulled back, inwardly cursing his lack of control when it came to Merrie.

"I am sorry," he murmured, looking down upon her flushed face. "I have taken advantage of your kindness again."

"I—I don't mind," she said, blinking back her surprise at his apology. "I mean, you're not taking advantage. I—I liked it...I mean, your kiss. I wanted you to kiss me. I—I want you."

Griffin quickly got to his feet and stepped away from the couch, putting a reasonable distance between them. "My behavior was unseemly. And for that, I am truly sorry." He rubbed his palms together and forced a smile. "I believe I might take a walk."

She stood and stepped in front of him, blocking his retreat to the door with her body. "I'm not some naive schoolgirl!" she snapped. "I was a willing participant. This is the twentieth century, Griffin, and it takes two to tango. No one," she continued, punctuating her words with a poke to his chest, "and I mean no one kisses me unless I *want* to be kissed." With that, she turned and stalked to her bedroom, slamming the door behind her.

Griffin frowned, completely confused by her outburst. He drew a deep breath, trying to still his thudding heart and the urge to follow her. Damn, she was inviting his touch, craving his advances! He knew of her low moral character, yet he couldn't bring himself to take advantage. What kind of man had he become that he couldn't make love to a woman with Merrie's beauty and obvious passions?

He glanced over at Ben Gunn who sat silently on his perch, watching him with a suspicious, unblinking eye. "I believe I have put myself in the doghouse again," he said to the gray parrot.

"Have a care," Ben said.

"Fine advice," Griffin replied. He shifted on his feet, wincing at the blatant proof of his arousal and willing himself to relax. "Perhaps a walk would be just the thing right now."

5

TO MEREDITH'S GREAT RELIEF, the next day dawned bright and clear and the weather promised to hold for at least the next five days. After their disastrous kiss the previous afternoon, she'd done all she could to avoid Griffin. She was as anxious as he was to get the trip under way and leave the embarrassment of her feeble attempts at seduction far behind.

What had ever made her think she might be able to entice him into something more than what they had? He'd slept beside her twice, yet he'd not made any move to seduce *her*. And every kiss they'd shared could be construed as nothing more than an expression of gratitude. Griffin Rourke didn't find her attractive in the least.

To keep her mind off her mortification, she began to make preparations for their trip to Bath the next day. Griffin walked with her down to the harbor to take a look at the small sailboat she had chartered, excited about the prospect of getting off the island. He made no mention of what had happened between them the previous afternoon and Meredith was convinced that he, too, wanted to forget.

While he examined the layout of the lines, she went to Jenny's General Store, a rambling white clapboard building on the water, for provisions for their trip.

A long porch shaded the side entrance, and the two rocking chairs and low bench were occupied with the usual morning group. Jenny's husband, the balding Hubey

Hogue, had commandeered the head rocker. Early Jackson, the wiry, wizened owner of Happy Jack's Fishing Charters sat in the other rocker. Two younger members of the group, the bespectacled Lyle Burleswell and the flame-haired Shep Cummings, rounded out the group. Lyle owned the Sandpiper Hotel and Shep was the island's venerable handyman. They all sipped coffee out of a motley collection of chipped mugs, while they munched donuts and kept an eye on passersby on both the road and in the harbor.

"Morning, Meredith." Early tipped his captain's cap. "Hear you're chartering a sailboat for tomorrow."

Meredith smiled. The only way to keep a secret on Ocracoke Island was to take a vacation to the mainland. Even then, the rampant speculation about the trip was worse than whatever secret a person was trying to keep.

"Taking a trip to Bath," Hubey commented.

"With her friend," Lyle added.

"Griffin Rourke," Shep completed.

They all spoke as if their own particular revelation was the most startling. Tabloid television had nothing over the porch at Jenny's General Store. Even the most mundane subjects became exciting fodder for the island news service.

Meredith stepped up on the porch. "That's right. We're leaving at—"

"Dawn," Early said. "Weather's supposed to be just fine. No hurricanes in the forecast."

Lyle nodded. "We all know how you're bothered by bad weather," he said sympathetically.

"But it looks like you survived Horace with no worries," Shep said.

"But then, that was only a category one," Hubey concluded. "Nothing like Delia."

"I have some shopping to do," Meredith said as she reached for the screen door, anxious to escape the inquisition.

"Hey, we heard your boyfriend might be looking for work," Hubey said.

Meredith froze, her hand on the door. "What?"

"Yeah," Early said. "Tank Muldoon says your Griffin was asking about jobs on the island when he was in there a few days back."

"I guess Rourke's planning to stick around for a while," Lyle said.

Shep shook his head. "Jobs are hard to come by on the island."

"You tell your friend, Griffin, to come down to our dock as soon as you get back from your trip," Early said. "Me and the boys bought ourselves an old shrimper. We're going to haul it out and fix it up and sell it to a guy down Georgia way. If Rourke ain't scared of hard work, we can give him something to do and pay him for it."

"I—I'll tell him that. Thank you." Meredith quickly stepped inside the dim, cool interior of the store. Overhead, fans gently whirred from the low ceiling, mixing the smells of meat and produce with the salt air. Shelves stacked high with goods ran the length of the building, separated by narrow aisles. The old wooden floor creaked beneath her feet as she reached for a plastic basket from the stack beside the door.

Early's words echoed in her mind and she tried to fathom their meaning. Had Griffin finally resigned himself to staying? She shook her head. No, it couldn't be. Early had misunderstood. If Griffin had decided to stay, she would have been the first to know. She brushed the thought from her mind and focused on her shopping list.

"'Mornin', Meredith," Jenny called from behind the register. "Hear your boyfriend is looking for a job."

Startled, Meredith snatched a can of tuna and tossed it in her basket, then glanced over at Jenny. The storekeeper peered at her through the reading glasses perched on the end of her nose, a newspaper propped up in front of her. "Yes . . . he is," Meredith called.

She moved down the aisle, picked up a box of taco shells and studied the nutritional label distractedly.

"So, are you two planning to stay on the island for a while?"

"No," Meredith said, shoving the box back on the shelf and continuing down the aisle. "I mean, I'll be here through December, but I'm not sure how long Griffin will be staying." She peeked around the whole-wheat dinner rolls to find Jenny staring at her, a concerned frown wrinkling her forehead.

"You two having problems? Tank says your Griffin was hoisting a few the other night at his place. Said he was in the doghouse."

Meredith groaned inwardly. Living on this island was like having a hundred sets of nosy parents. From the day she'd set foot on Ocracoke again, she'd become part of a larger family, filled with people who had helped her father raise her all those years ago. Hubey and Jenny had given her her first after-school job. Early's wife, Millie, had taught her how to iron Sam Abbott's shirts. Lyle had lent her his collection of Civil War history books and Shep had teased her mercilessly from the time they'd entered the first grade together.

So how could she be angry with their prying? After all, they cared about her happiness. "Griffin and I are getting along just fine," Meredith said with a smile. *Too* fine, if the truth be told.

Her thoughts wandered back to the kiss they'd shared on her couch. She'd recalled the moment again and again, each time, searching for some clue to his true feelings. But her limited experience in the ways of passion gave her a distinct disadvantage.

She was nearly certain she'd seen desire suffuse his expression the instant before he kissed her. But then, it could have been boredom. And the kiss itself had been incredibly wonderful, deep and soul shattering, to say the least. But then, *he* had drawn away with some ridiculous excuse about unseemly behavior and taking a walk. Suddenly, she wasn't quite sure what had happened between them.

One thing she did know was that the man knew how to kiss. When their lips had touched, she'd felt as if every ounce of his attention was focused on her mouth, his firm lips tempting her, his tongue offering her a taste of his soul. And his body... all that hard muscle and warm sinew, as though he'd been carved from sun-warmed granite...

"He is a handsome young man," Jenny called, "even if his hair is a bit long."

Meredith swallowed convulsively. "Yes," she said, her voice catching in her throat. "Yes, he is. Do you think he needs a haircut?"

Jenny pondered the question for a moment, then smiled slyly. "Naw. He looks mighty fine just the way he is." With that, thankfully, Jenny went back to her crossword puzzle and left Meredith to her shopping... and her fantasies.

She silently chastised herself. This would have to stop! She couldn't walk around all moony-eyed over the man. Griffin had made it perfectly clear that he would do everything in his power to get back to his own time. For days, he'd refused to consider the other alternative.

But she couldn't put Early's words out of her head. If they were true, maybe Griffin had changed his mind. Could he be responding to the undeniable attraction between them?

As Meredith grabbed a bag of mini-marshmallows, she attempted to ignore the blooming optimism that flooded her heart. She would not allow herself a single instant of hope. There couldn't be a future for them... especially after he learned that she might be the one responsible for bringing him here in the first place.

So Tank had told Early, she mused, quickly forgetting her resolve. And Griffin had told Tank he was looking for work—before Meredith had told Griffin that Kelsey had told *her* that there might be a way for Griffin to get home. Meredith stopped in the middle of the produce section, dizzy from trying to sort out all the conversational connections.

Maybe she would do well to put the whole matter out of her mind. The fact was, as long as Griffin had hope, he would try to return. And as long as he stayed, she, too, would harbor a hope of her own. But for now, she'd have to keep her hope, and her fantasies, in check.

Ten minutes later, Meredith made her way to the tiny marina, a grocery bag clutched in each arm. As she walked down the dock, she caught sight of Griffin sitting in the cockpit of the twenty-five-foot sloop they'd rented. His attention was focused on a navigational chart he held out in front of him.

She stopped and slowly placed the bags on the dock, then straightened, her gaze coming to rest on Griffin. He was a devastatingly handsome man, there was no denying that fact. And Jenny hadn't been the only one on the island to notice. He'd elicited a number of appreciative stares, from sixteen-year-old schoolgirls to gray-haired grandmothers.

She watched as he brushed his wind-whipped hair back from his face, revealing a startlingly perfect profile. How could any woman help staring? His dark, brooding good looks were like a magnet to the eyes. She'd caught herself watching him so many times over the past few days, wondering whether she really knew him at all, or whether he was as he appeared—an enigma.

Even if he stayed, he'd never lack for feminine companionship. Merrie's heart twisted at the thought and all her self-confidence drained out of her body. How could she have thought she'd be able to hold his interest? She was a shy, boring history professor who had never been able to attract much more than a mild interest from the opposite sex.

"Too bookish" had been used to describe her on more than one occasion, and that came from men who spent just as much time with their books as she did! The descriptive "cold fish" and the ever-popular "painfully proper" had also been applied to her, according to Kelsey.

Meredith sighed. He was grateful for her help, and that was the limit of his feelings for her. She hadn't seen desire in his eyes, she'd seen gratitude. And all his talk about honor was simply a smoke screen so he wouldn't have to kiss her again!

He didn't find her sexually attractive in the least. She had waited for him each night, hoping that he'd need comfort and come to her. But when she awoke at dawn, she found the other side of her bed cold and empty. With a body as unremarkable as hers, was it any wonder he had thought she was a boy that first night?

"Merrie-girl!"

Meredith blinked hard, bringing her thoughts back to the present. She forced a smile and waved at Griffin, suddenly uneasy in his presence. Could he tell she'd been thinking of him?

He stood up in the cockpit. "She is a fine little sloop. With this boat, I could sail across the Atlantic and back by myself!"

"We're going to Bath," Meredith said, "and no farther."

He sent her a powerful smile and her knees grew weak. "Ah, but Merrie, I would show you the world, if I could. Come on board, and we'll sail away this very moment."

At his casual words, a tremble of uncontrolled regret shook her to the core. If only it were so simple. If only he wanted her. But no matter how far they sailed, nothing would change the fact that they were simply friends, two strangers who had been thrown together by fate.

"Come, Merrie, let's take a sail around the harbor. I need to practice."

With a hesitant nod, she picked up the groceries and headed toward the boat. Griffin deftly leaped onto the dock and took both bags from her arms, then helped her into the cockpit.

"All right," Merrie said. "You're the captain."

"And you'll make a fine first mate, Merrie-girl. Now, go forward and cast off that line for me."

Meredith arched her eyebrow at his suddenly stern manner, then did as she was told. Today, they would sail for fun. But tomorrow, they would sail to Bath, and once again they would try to find a way for him to return to his own time.

And if they succeeded, Griffin would be gone from her life. Forever.

THE SALT BREEZE skimmed across the water, kicking up sprightly whitecaps on the blue surface of the wide Pamlico River. Mare's-tail clouds trailed across the azure sky, the colors a reflection of the sea below, where their white-sailed sloop sliced through the water.

Meredith sat in the cockpit and watched Griffin steer the boat before the brisk wind. They'd been on the water since sunrise, sailing across the Sound and up the Pamlico River. After their sail around the harbor the previous afternoon, Griffin had easily adjusted to the new technology of the sloop, instinctively knowing which lines controlled which functions. She was right—sailing hadn't changed much in the nearly three hundred years that stood between them. But then, Griffin had spent most of his life on the water.

They passed the time in idle conversation, Meredith relating stories of the breezy days she'd spent on her father's shrimp boat, wrapped in a blanket, her nose stuck in a history book; and the sunny days they'd spent in the harbor, her father teaching her to navigate the little sailboat he'd built for her. He'd been a man who loved the water and she had inherited his fascination with all things seaworthy. But like her father, she was wary of the weather, always keeping one eye on the horizon, ready for the worst.

She had hoped that talk of her life would encourage Griffin to speak of his own. She knew of his father and mother, but was still left to wonder just who Griffin Rourke really was.

Meredith sighed inwardly and stared up at the sky, watching a gull dip and sway on the wind. Though the day hadn't been conducive to enlightening conversation, at least it was perfect for sailing. Out on the Sound, she had bundled up against the wind. But once they reached the sheltered waters of the Pamlico River, the afternoon sun had warmed her. They ate a picnic lunch while still under sail near Pamlico Point, the place where the river emptied into the Sound.

It was nearly dinnertime when they made the turn into Bath Creek, a wide tributary more aptly compared to a river than a stream. The shallow draft of the sloop made navigating simple, but Meredith kept her eyes on the charts, anyway. The colonial town sat on the water's edge, much as it had in the early 1700s, when it served as the first port of entry and the seat of colonial government in North Carolina.

Griffin seemed suddenly still, staring beyond the bow of the boat at the small waterside town. The breeze fluttered in his hair, the only sign that he was a mortal man and not some marble likeness of an ancient sea god.

"Do you recognize anything?" she asked softly.

He nodded slowly. "Some. The shoreline looks a bit changed."

"More than a few storms have roared through here in the past three centuries," she explained.

"There are more houses in some places and less in others, but they have changed also." He cocked his head toward the bridge that spanned the creek ahead of them. "And that wasn't there."

"None of the structures from your time have survived. But there are some clues that have been found." She pointed off to the starboard. "Blackbeard had a home over there, on Plum Point, isn't that right?"

He nodded again, silently studying the wooded area. "He has built himself a fine home, for a pirate," Griffin murmured, as if he could see the house in his mind's eye. "Teach fancies himself quite a gentlemen. He hosts lavish entertainments at his home. And he boasts that there is not a home in the colony to which he wouldn't be welcome for dinner." The last was said with more than a trace of bitterness.

She found it so strange to hear him speak of Blackbeard as if the man were still alive. He didn't say much, but Meredith could see his anger toward the pirate simmering near the surface. Still, she felt a familiar sense of satisfaction in his simple explanation, the same feeling she had when she found an original source to confirm one of her historical suppositions. Everything he'd told her so far had slipped into the annals of history without much dispute.

Suddenly, she wanted to know everything she could about Blackbeard. If speaking of the pirate might keep Griffin here longer, then so be it. She would ask all the questions she wanted, without guilt or remorse. And her book would be better for Griffin's time here.

She would write down everything she told him and they would talk for hours about his experience. And then, when all the questions had been asked, she would know that he had been brought forward to help with her work and not to encourage her fantasy. But would he then disappear from her life? Or had Griffin Rourke been brought here to stay?

"There is a depression in the ground, right over there," she said. "And ruins from a foundation. And in a shallow field between the point and Bath, there was a round brick oven which we think was used by Blackbeard to boil tar for caulking his ships."

"I know the oven you speak of," he said distractedly. "I have seen it many times. When the tar boils, it can be smelled for miles."

"It's not there anymore. So many tourists came to visit it, they trampled the farmer's field, so he covered the oven with dirt and plowed it over. You can also see the ruins of the foundation of Governor Eden's house over there." She pointed across the port side.

"This seems familiar, the land and the water, yet it is not."

"Do you think you can find the place where you fell in?"

"It is here," he said.

"Here?" Meredith asked.

Griffin moved to drop the sails. She scrambled to the bow and grabbed hold of the anchor and heaved it in, playing out the line until she felt the anchor hit bottom. The boat drifted and then slowly stopped as the anchor held. As she crawled back to the cockpit, she saw Griffin smiling at her.

"Why didn't you say something? I didn't realize this was the place that..." A rush of warmth flooded her body and for a brief instant, she lost herself in his pale blue eyes. "What?" she asked.

"What?"

"You're laughing at me," she said, the warmth now flushing her face.

"You are a fine sailor, Merrie."

"You find that odd?"

"For a woman. I find your sailing talents quite...useful, practical."

She glanced up at him. "Thank you for the roundabout compliment, Captain Rourke. And that has been my life's goal, to prove myself useful to a man."

He groaned and shook his head. "You have misunderstood me again. I also find it admirable. You are a woman of many talents, Merrie."

She jumped to her feet and dropped a mocking curtsy, then sat down again. "Aye, Captain, that I am."

Griffin secured the tiller then took a seat across from her. His gaze drifted past her, over the water to the town. "I know Bath Town as a much rougher place," he said. "It looks almost deserted now."

"The big ships don't come in here anymore, so there isn't much commerce—just a fine collection of historic houses, a lovely old church and about two hundred people. But I think it's one of the most beautiful and serene places in North Carolina. I've come here many times while researching my—" She stopped herself, realizing she'd nearly mentioned her book on Blackbeard. "Researching," she repeating.

"Well, we might as well be about our business now before the sun goes down." Griffin reached down and tugged off his deck shoes. Then he stood up and stripped off his shirt.

His chest gleamed under the late afternoon light, rippled muscle and hard flesh. Her fingers clenched spasmodically as she remembered her exploration of his body the last time he'd come to her bed. How she had wanted to touch him, to prove to herself that he was a flesh-and-blood man, a man who would respond to her touch, and not just the fantasy hero of her dreams.

He reached for the waistband of his trousers. She gulped hard. "Wha—what are you doing?"

"I'm going to get wet, Merrie-girl, the same way I did that night. Turn your head. I would not want to offend your tender sensibilities."

He tugged the trousers down along his narrow hips and she quickly closed her eyes.

"You can't just take off all your clothes and jump in!" she cried.

"And why not? If I can wear a dress on the main street of Ocracoke Village, certainly my nakedness in the middle of Old Town Creek would not cause eyebrows to rise."

She felt the boat rock slightly and then heard a splash. Slowly, she opened her eyes and peered overboard. He broke the surface right under her nose, water sluicing over his shoulders. Tiny droplets clung to his dark lashes, like diamond chips, and she found herself suddenly unable to catch her breath.

"Brrr, it's cold," he growled, shaking his head and scattering the diamonds across the blue water.

Lord, he was glorious, and even more so without clothes. She cursed her cowardice. She should have looked when she'd had the chance. After all, just when *was* the last time she'd seen a naked man. An image came to mind and she winced. The sight of Griffin in the buff would easily supplant *that* memory.

She tried to make out the details of his body through the wavering water, but then he kicked away and swam out from the boat with strong, sure strokes, his shoulder and feet breaking the surface. For a moment, she glimpsed his bare backside and the line at his waist that marked his deeply tanned back.

He stopped swimming about twenty yards from the boat, then turned back to look at her, lazily treading water as if he hadn't exerted himself in the least. "Well?" he called.

"Well what?" she replied. Did he want her to comment on his swimming skills or was he waiting for her to swoon at the sight of his naked body?

"This is the place and the time is about right," he said. "Do you see anything?"

"Not as much as I'd like to see," she muttered softly.

"What?" he called, frowning at her.

"What am I supposed to see?" she called. "What did you see that night?"

"I don't know. I was standing at the rail of the *Adventure* and I thought I heard someone behind me. I turned, and the next thing I knew, I was in your house, trussed up on your sofa."

"Well, maybe you should just swim around for a while," Meredith suggested. "Slowly," she added.

He did as he was told, circling the boat in a lazy crawl, his rippled back glinting wet in the diminishing light. She watched him for a long time, soaking up the sight of his nude body as it slipped through the water. The sun dipped lower on the horizon and then, in a red blaze, set behind the remains of Thistleworth Plantation, the home of the duplicitous Eden, friend to Blackbeard.

He stopped swimming a few yards from the boat, then brushed his wet hair back from his face. "Nothing is happening," he said.

"How do you feel?" Meredith asked.

She thought she heard him curse. He looked up at her. "Cold, wet, and nothing more."

Disappointment colored his voice and frustration was evident in his eyes.

"Maybe you should come back on board."

He glanced around once more, waiting, watching, then shrugged resignedly. With a knifelike movement, he kicked his feet out and submerged.

"I'm sorry, Griffin," she murmured. "But we tried."

Meredith waited for him to surface, but after fifteen seconds, he still hadn't come up for air. Thirty seconds passed, then sixty, and still he didn't come up.

Meredith leaned over the combing and looked into the water. "Griffin?" she called. "Griffin!" The last was a desperate shout, her voice echoing across the width of the river. A clock ticked in her head, multiplying her anxiety with each second he remained underwater.

Suddenly, a pair of wet arms circled her from behind. She screamed and twisted against the embrace. Griffin's deep chuckle sounded in her ear, sending a warm shudder through her body. "So ye thought I drowned, did ye?"

"Let go of me!" Meredith protested. "You're wet! And cold!"

He pulled her against him playfully, and she felt the subtle imprint of his body along her spine and backside. She squirmed in his arms until she faced him, then looked up into his eyes. Suddenly, the teasing smile faded from his face.

He bent his head and covered her mouth with his, his kiss swift and intense, his tongue plumbing the depths of her mouth until she felt as if she might lose consciousness.

She returned his kiss in full measure, running her hands along his damp chest and twisting them around his neck. He moaned deep in his throat and drew her hard against him until she could feel his desire spring up against her belly.

He *did* want her! Her heart sang and her senses whirled with the realization. Whether he was ready to admit it or not, he felt the same passion for her as she did for him! And at that moment, she realized that he had been brought here for a reason—to fulfill her fantasies.

Then, just as quickly as he'd covered her mouth with his, he drew back. He closed his eyes and slowly shook his head. "Damn, Merrie, you sorely tempt me," he whispered. "You must not allow this to happen again."

"Me?" she asked, breathless. "I—I don't understand."

"Do not ask me why, for I am not sure I would be able to explain. Call it a point of honor. I know you've encountered scoundrels in your past and I will not be counted among them. Your reputation will not be sullied any further than it already has."

"Sully?" Meredith blinked hard and stared up at him, completely baffled by his words. Though she didn't know much about men, she certainly knew that sleeping together in the same bed was worth more "sully" points than a simple kiss! Sure, he *was* naked now, but his state of undress didn't even enter into the picture. If he was worried about her reputation, he should have stayed out of her bedroom, not out of her arms.

"You are a passionate woman, Merrie, a woman of . . . worldly experience. And I know this will be difficult for you, but we must not allow ourselves these pleasures."

"Why not?" Meredith said quietly.

"I must leave you someday. I'm not sure when, but I vow I will not leave you with regret."

Meredith spun out of his grasp and snatched his trousers, then held them over her shoulder. "You'd better put on your pants." After he took them from her, she made her way back to the cockpit. She stared out over the water and considered his words.

If he was truly brought here to fulfill her fantasies, then why was he so determined to push her away? Why couldn't he give in to the feelings that were so obviously growing between them?

They'd almost exhausted their options. Until they figured out what had happened, and why, they were merely guessing at a method to return him to his own time.

Meredith closed her eyes and hugged her arms to her chest. If he'd been brought here to help in her research, maybe she ought to question him, to find out everything she could. Once that was done, maybe he'd be free to return.

And if Griffin had been brought here to make her fantasies a reality, to rid her of her virginity, the fastest way to solve that problem would be to—

She snapped her eyes open and bit back a groan. Maybe he'd been brought here to *torment* her. For if her work and her virginity were at stake, she wasn't quite sure she'd be willing to give him up for either! Though he wanted to return to exact his plan against Blackbeard, she couldn't help hoping that he'd stay, that he wouldn't find a way back.

Meredith cursed softly. So what was she to do? How was she to know the right course to take?

"Merrie? Are you all right?"

She shivered and rubbed her forearms, her eyes still fixed on a fisherman who was dangling a line off the bridge. "Are you dressed?" she asked.

"I would not have thought you such a Puritan, Merrie," he teased, trying to lighten the mood between them. He was acting as if nothing had happened between them at all. "You show your ankles, and even your knees, in public all the time."

"That's different." She turned around. "You shouldn't have scared me like that," she murmured. "I thought you'd drowned. And how did you sneak on board? The boat didn't even rock."

"An old pirate trick," he said. "Serves me well, don't you think?"

She forced a smile, trying hard to return his lighthearted banter, but her heart wasn't in it. "And have you crept on board many boats, wearing nothing but a smile, to accost women?"

He frowned in mock pensiveness, then grinned, the corners of his mouth curling up in a charming way. "Many, many women, Merrie-girl. But not a one quite like you."

Meredith stared at him, her gaze locked on his. She reached out and gently placed her palm on his bare chest, brushing away the moist sheen of river water. A frisson of heat stole though her fingers and up her arm, but she didn't pull away. "I'm sorry it didn't work, Griffin. Maybe we just didn't find the right place." But she wasn't truly sorry, for anything that kept Griffin with her could only make her happy.

"Perhaps," he said. "Yet I am beginning to wonder if we ever will find the end to this tangle."

"We will," she said, not really believing in the truth of her words. Meredith drew a deep breath. "I'm hungry. We can eat on board or we can row the dinghy to shore. There's an inn that serves dinner and we can spend the night there, if you like."

"I would rather stay on the water," he said. "I feel more at home out here."

Meredith watched as he made his way back to the bow. For a moment, things had become so simple between them, two people sharing a moment of passion. But then, the past sprang up like a great sea monster, rocking the boat and upsetting the easy balance they'd achieved...and reminding her that, no matter how much she wanted it, there was still a very good chance that Griffin would never be hers.

THE FIRST SIGNS of dawn colored the eastern horizon a soft pink, bathing the landscape in an otherworldly light. Distant calls of waking birds echoed across the dark surface of the creek, their songs accompanied by the gentle slap of the water on the side of the boat. Griffin stood on the bow of the small sailboat, his gaze fixed on the twinkling lights from Bath Town, his fingers wrapped around the jib stay.

Merrie was sound asleep in the tiny cabin below, curled up in the port bunk. Though he'd tried, he couldn't sleep. He'd thought about crawling into the berth beside her and pulling her pliant body against his. With her close, maybe he could forget the demons that plagued his mind and find a few hours of rest.

But instead of taking shelter in her warmth, instinct told him to go back on deck, to watch and wait for some sign. He'd even dived in and circled the boat a few more times, hoping that he'd stumble upon a door to the past.

Griffin ran his fingers through his damp hair. The longer he stayed away, the more difficult it became to sustain his resolve. Somewhere, hidden deep in the past, the pirate Blackbeard waited. Yet now, the vision of Griffin's revenge seemed to be fading, as if a thick fog had descended on the past.

He stood on deck for a long time, watching the rising light glint off the water. His thoughts returned time and again to the woman who slept below, to her perfect face and her tempting body. And then, as if she'd been brought there by the sheer force of his will, he felt her presence behind him and he knew, without turning, that he was no longer alone.

Merrie stepped to his side, clutching a blanket around her shoulders against the damp morning breeze. "Are you all right?" she said. She placed her fingers on his arm and a surge of heat warmed his blood. "I woke up and you were gone."

"I didn't mean to frighten you," he replied, hearing the apprehension in her voice. She had thought he was gone, for good. Griffin cursed inwardly as guilt washed over him. For Merrie's sake, he had to find a way back. But though his mind was set on returning to his own time, he couldn't help wondering if what he was leaving was really what he was seeking . . . peace, a sense of well-being and the time to take a bit of joy from life.

That was all he really wanted. He'd been set on this course of revenge for nearly a year, without pause for anything, including his own happiness. And now, in this place and in this time, he'd found a brief respite, a few quiet moments to forget all that the pirate Blackbeard had wrought on his family.

"You're cold," she said. "Were you in the water again?"

He nodded distractedly as he stared at the shoreline. "In the dark, it almost looks right to me," he said. "I can nearly believe I'm there. I had a room at an inn that used to stand on that bit of land." Griffin pointed to the base of the bridge that now crossed Old Town Creek.

"It must be hard for you to be away from your home," she said.

Griffin shrugged. "My home is the sea, it always has been. And the sea hasn't changed at all in three hundred years."

"Haven't you ever thought about settling down? About marrying and having a family?"

He glanced at her, meeting her questioning gaze in the soft morning light. His sweet Merrie, always so direct, so interested in what was inside his mind and heart. "Once," Griffin replied, banishing the image of his son's tiny grave from his mind. "But then, it became clear that I did not deserve as much."

"I don't understand," Merrie said. "Why would you not deserve to be happy?"

"I live my life on my ship, Merrie. And a wife and family must stay on dry land. I would not make a good husband or a good father."

Meredith squeezed his arm. "Don't say that. How do you know until you've actually tried?"

Griffin turned his head and stared out toward the Pamlico. He should tell Merrie exactly how he knew. Yet speaking of his failure as a husband and father only brought back a rush of paralyzing guilt and pain. Merrie saw him as a good and honorable man, and what she believed of him mattered. "I know," he said softly, slipping his arm around her shoulder. He pulled her into the circle of his embrace and she wrapped her arms around his waist.

They stood that way for a long time, silently watching the sunrise, not needing to speak. Strange how he felt as if he'd known Merrie his whole life. They shared an inexplicable connection that transcended time and distance. Though he wanted to deny it, maybe destiny had thrown them together for a reason.

Griffin considered the notion for a moment. The theory made as much sense as any other explanation he had come up with. But then, perhaps he was simply trying to make excuses for himself, trying to find a reason to give up. Perhaps *he* controlled his own destiny and every errant thought of remaining with Merrie was putting him further from his task.

"I think you're wrong," she said softly.

"Wrong?"

"About being a good husband and father."

He laughed harshly. "You do not know me, Merrie. So don't make me into some mythical hero with a heart of purest gold."

"That's not what I meant," she replied. "But you are a good and honorable man."

He turned to her, probing her gaze with his. "Am I?"

"Yes," she replied.

Griffin reached out and ran a finger along her cheek. "Ah, Merrie-girl, you do *not* know me. If I am an honorable man, then why do I want to kiss you right now?"

She blinked in surprise. "I—I don't know," she murmured. "But maybe you should kiss me and find out."

Griffin shook his head. "You tempt me again, Merrie. Have a care or I will do precisely that."

She reached up and idly brushed his hair from his temple. "You're in my time, Griffin, not yours. And in the twentieth century, a kiss is just a kiss, and not a matter of honor."

"And because I am here, does that make me a different man?" he challenged. "For I do not feel different, not in my head nor in my heart. And you cannot expect me to live by your rules." Griffin took her shoulders and gave her a gentle shake. "I do want you, Merrie. Lord help me, I do. But to take you would be unfair, for I can promise you nothing in return."

She put her arms around his waist and pressed herself against his chest. "You—you wouldn't take me. I would give myself to you, Griffin. And I don't need any promises."

Griffin sighed. "I have set myself on a course and nothing can divert me. Though I do not know why I am still here, I must believe that I will return to my place in history to complete my task. And when I return, I will leave you here." He paused, then gently held her away from him. "I would not have you regret our time together."

The color rose in her cheeks and she turned away from him, pulling the blanket more tightly around her, as if it might offer some protection from his words.

Griffin hesitantly placed his hands on her shoulders. "If my presence is too difficult for you to take, I will leave."

"No!" she cried, spinning around to face him. "No," she repeated in a tremulous voice. "I understand, and I will respect your feelings. You don't have to leave."

Griffin smiled. "Good. For I have come to depend on you, Merrie, and I am afraid I may feel lost without your practical counsel."

She graced him with a halfhearted smile as he adjusted the blanket around her shoulders.

"We will be friends then," he said, tugging on the blanket playfully.

"Friends," she repeated in a small voice.

"And now, my sweet friend, I suggest you crawl into your berth and go back to sleep. The time has come to return to Ocracoke. I will get our little boat under way and when you awaken, we will have our breakfast." He gave Merrie a quick kiss on her forehead, then steered her toward the cabin.

After he'd tucked her in, Griffin came back on deck. But instead of lifting anchor, he stripped off his clothes once more and dived into the frigid water. With strong, even strokes, he swam around the boat, again and again, until his muscles ached and his pulse pounded.

Then, kicking his feet up, he dived for the bottom, digging through the dark water. He stayed submerged, waiting for the door to open, his breath burning in his chest. And when he couldn't hold his breath any longer, he shot to the surface, breaking into the sunlight, gasping for air.

As he floated on his back, exhausted, he stared up at the sky. For the first time since he'd come to this century, he had good cause to believe he might never get back home.

6

"NO LEECHES!"

Meredith glared at Griffin as he sat on the end of Dr. Kincaid's examining table. The nurse had shown them in a few minutes before and ordered Griffin to remove his shirt. She gave him an appreciative once-over before she popped a thermometer into his mouth and left the room, leaving Meredith alone to ponder the play of muscles across his shoulders and chest.

Meredith had thought it best to accompany Griffin, considering his rather low opinion of the medical profession. Apparently, the only doctor Griffin had ever encountered had used some rather primitive medical practices, including the curative use of bloodsucking worms.

"Put that thermometer back in your mouth," Meredith said.

He stuck it under his tongue with a stubborn expression. "Ummph!" he replied. "Ut about da eeches?"

"Do you see any leeches?" she asked impatiently. Lord, he was going to drive her mad. He'd been prowling the cottage for the past few days, even surlier than he'd been before, coughing and sniffling and ignoring his symptoms as if giving in to them would be less than manly. She'd offered him aspirin, cold tablets, cough medicine, but he'd preferred whiskey, straight up. "Forget the leeches," she said.

Griffin grumbled an unintelligible response, then snatched the thermometer from his mouth. "The butcher will bleed me, then. 'Tis the same thing. Always with them 'tis bad blood. They should stick to what they do best, cutting hair."

She placed a hand on his upper arm to calm him, then hesitantly pulled it away as a flood of warmth raced up her arm. If she knew what was good for her, she'd make it a point not to allow herself the pleasure of touching him, especially when they were alone in a room with him half-dressed. "I promise you," she said, "this doctor will not bleed you, or cut your hair. He'll give you some medicine to help your cold."

"But I am not cold."

"You *have* a cold, or the ague, as you call it. I think you might have a bronchial infection—"

"Lung fever," Griffin corrected, slapping his broad chest with his palm. "I know what ails me and I know how to cure it. A mustard poultice and a few drams of good whiskey."

Her gaze wandered to his hand as he idly rubbed his palm on his chest. Meredith, mesmerized, imagined her fingers doing the same, furrowing through the silky dark hair, drifting over the hard muscle and smooth skin. With a sharp breath, she glanced up at his face. "If you have an infection, the doctor will give you some antibiotics and you'll be fine," she said, her voice a bit uneven.

She drew a long breath. At first, she thought Griffin had just caught a common cold, a result of his midnight swim in Bath Creek, but then she realized he was stoically fighting something more. When she finally managed to force a thermometer between his teeth, she found a low-grade fever. It was then she realized that Griffin was probably at risk for any number of modern diseases and mutated germs.

"If I were you, I wouldn't mention the leeches again," Meredith said. "Just let me answer any questions the doctor asks."

"I can speak for myself," Griffin countered, putting the thermometer back into his mouth as if to signal the end of the discussion.

The door to the examining room opened and a woman in a white lab coat walked in. She held out her hand to Meredith. "I'm Dr. Susan McMillan. I'm taking care of Doc Kincaid's patients while he's on vacation. I usually work out of the medical center in Kitty Hawk." She held out her hand to Griffin, as well. Griffin glanced at Meredith before mimicking her handshake.

She knew what he was thinking. A doctor was bad enough, but a woman physician was guaranteed to arouse suspicion.

Dr. McMillan pulled the thermometer from Griffin's mouth. "What seems to be the problem, Mr. Rourke?"

"Griffin," he said. A smile quirked the corners of his mouth. "Or Griff, if you prefer."

Dr. McMillan took a deep breath and blinked hard, obviously not immune to Griffin's infectious smile, but apparently shocked that he'd be so blatant about it. Meredith bit back a laugh. If he thought he'd be able to charm his way out of an exam, he had another guess coming.

"Griff," Dr. McMillan repeated. "What is the problem, then?"

"The problem is, I don't want to be here," he said in a seductive tone. "Merrie believes me to be ill, but as you can see I am in perfect health."

"I think he has a chest cold," Meredith amended. "He's had it for about a week. And now, I think it might be developing into a bronchial infection. He's been coughing a lot and running a low-grade fever for the past three days."

"His temperature is elevated," the doctor remarked. She adjusted her stethoscope and placed it on Griffin's naked chest. He jumped at her touch and she looked up at him in concern. "A little cold?" she asked.

He nodded. "That's what Merrie calls it, but I told her I don't feel cold. 'Tis lung fever. Or the ague." He watched the stethoscope suspiciously, frowning. To Meredith's relief, Dr. McMillan was listening more to Griffin's breathing than his self-diagnosis.

"Breathe in," she ordered. "Deep breath."

He did as he was told, over and over again, and Meredith watched the rise and fall of his chest. What if it was something more than just a cold? He could have tuberculosis or some other disease that he'd brought with him. Meredith clasped her hands in front of her, twisting her fingers together. She couldn't bear it if she'd brought him here only for him to succumb to some twentieth-century illness.

When the doctor finished listening to his breathing, she pulled out a tongue depressor and held it up to his mouth. He drew back and stared at the flat stick as if the woman were holding a dead fish to his nose.

"Open," she said.

"You expect me to eat that?" he asked. He gave Meredith a knowing glance, as if the medicinal properties of eating a piece of wood were well known, even to his colonial mind.

"Open your mouth," Meredith said, arching her eyebrow.

Hesitantly, he parted his lips.

"Open wide," Dr. McMillan said. As soon as she touched his tongue with the depressor, he pulled back. She looked at him in amusement. "I know most people hate the way it feels, but I need to see what's happening down there."

Dr. McMillan methodically proceeded to look into Griffin's throat, nose and ears, all the while dealing with his reluctant behavior. After she'd finished, she scribbled a few notes in the file, then turned to Griffin. "You do have a lot of congestion in your chest. We'll try a normal course of antibiotics and if it doesn't clear up, I'd like to do a chest X ray and a few more tests. I'll give you an injection right now and some tablets to take for the next ten days. I want you to be sure to take the entire course of medication. I'll be right back."

Meredith winced. An injection? If Griffin balked at the tongue depressor, he surely wouldn't care for a needle. She silently watched as the doctor left the room.

"She's not going to bleed me?" he whispered once she left.

"Griff?" Meredith asked, ignoring his question. "I could have told you that flirting with her wouldn't help, *Griff*. Maybe things are different in your time, but these days, doctors don't mess around with their patients."

"You sound like a jealous harpy, Merrie-girl," he teased.

"I'm not jealous! I just don't want you to make a fool of yourself. People will begin to ask questions that neither you nor I are prepared to answer."

"I never play the fool," he said, turning his smile on her.

She paused. "Then I better warn you now. She's going to give you a shot. But don't worry. Though it might look a little scary, it's really nothing. Children have them all the time."

"Scary?" Griffin asked.

"Well, there's a needle. And she'll inject some medicine into your arm, or maybe your backside, but—"

"What?" Griffin shouted.

"Trust me, it will only hurt for a second and it will help you get rid of that cough. A man who has taken to piracy for a hobby should not be afraid of a little old needle."

Griffin grabbed his shirt and pulled it on. "We are leaving now. I have been poked enough for one day and I have no intention of continuing the torture."

"Sorry for the wait!" Dr. McMillan breezed into the room. She stepped beside Griffin, and before he could protest, dabbed alcohol on his arm and jabbed him with the needle. He cursed vividly and pulled away, but it was all over quickly. Griffin was merely left to stare at his left arm in confusion. Strangely, the doctor was doing the same. She rubbed his upper arm with her thumb, examining it closely.

"You have no smallpox scar."

"I have managed to avoid that particular plague in my lifetime," Griffin murmured.

"No, I mean the scar from the vaccination."

"I—I don't believe Griffin had thé normal vaccinations," Meredith said. "He had a rather . . . unusual childhood. Maybe you could give him the full set of shots now?"

Griffin snapped his head up and glared at her. "I don't believe that's necessary," he said.

"It would be no trouble," Dr. McMillan said. "And even if you've had the vaccinations before, there would be no harm."

"Give him the whole list," Meredith said. "Whatever he needs. Smallpox, measles, polio, diphtheria."

The doctor nodded. "I can give him all the usual childhood vaccines, but I'm afraid we don't give a vaccination for smallpox anymore. The disease has been eradicated in this country, and in most of the world. If you plan to travel to some exotic locale, you'll need one for yellow fever, though."

"Yellow fever?" Griffin asked. "You have a needle to prevent yellow fever?"

"Yes," Dr. McMillan replied. "But I don't keep all those vaccines here. I'll need to send to the mainland for them. We can schedule another appointment. By that time, his fever will be gone and there won't be any problem administering the vaccines," she said to Meredith.

"And after you poke me with this needle, I will not get the fever?"

"Not for at least ten years," the doctor said. "You can put your shirt back on and I'll tell Linda to schedule another appointment for you next week."

Meredith stood and grabbed Griffin's arm as Dr. McMillan walked out of the examining room. "Thank you, Doctor."

Griffin stared after her, as if his mind were a million miles, or three hundred years, away. He silently followed Meredith out of the room and waited while she made another appointment. Finally, they stepped out onto the shaded porch of the tiny raised cottage that housed the island's health center. He still hadn't said anything and she suspected he was angry again.

"I'm sorry if the shot hurt you, but it's for your own good."

Griffin strode down the porch steps and headed across the sandy parking area.

Meredith ran after him, falling into step at his side. "All right, you can be mad if you like, but I was only looking out for your best interests. And just because I made an appointment for next week, doesn't mean that I believe you're going to be here. In fact, I'm doing this because I *know* you'll be going back."

He looked at her distractedly. "What?"

"Well, if you get these vaccines, it will protect you. When you go back—and please note that I said when, not if—at least I'll know that you won't die of some disease that could have been prevented. I—I guess it would make me feel better to know that you're healthy... and alive."

"That is very thoughtful of you, Merrie-girl," he said. Pausing, he drew a deep breath and forced a smile. "I have a taste for some of Mr. Muldoon's crab cakes. I think we should have lunch."

"Why won't you talk to me?" Meredith asked in frustration. "Whenever you seem bothered by something, you bottle it up inside. There is nothing wrong with expressing your feelings. It doesn't make you any less a man."

"Nothing is bothering me," he said with a shrug, continuing down the road.

Neither of them spoke again until the waitress had seated them on the deck of the Pirate's Cove, overlooking the tiny harbor. She greeted Meredith warmly and gave Griffin an appreciative glance, then placed a menu in front of them.

Griffin studied the menu intently, then dropped it to the table and sighed. "It is not something I find simple," he replied. "You seem to want to speak of everything, leaving nothing to private contemplation."

"That's not it," Meredith said, picking up the conversation as if there had been no lull at all. "It's just that we've been living together for nearly two weeks and I know very little about you. If we were truly friends, then you would talk to me."

"I could drink a pint of ale right now," Griffin said, looking out across the water.

"You're doing it again," Meredith said.

"It seems I'm not hungry, after all," Griffin said, pushing to his feet.

Meredith rolled her eyes at the waitress's questioning look. Griffin stood next to the table for a moment, waiting for her to get up, but she stubbornly picked up her menu and studied it.

"I'm hungry," she said, "and I'm going to have some lunch. You can join me and we'll talk, or you can find a nice quiet place and spend the rest of your afternoon in brooding solitude."

"All right," he said, sinking into the chair across from her. The waitress hurried over and took their orders before Griffin had another chance to escape, then brought them two mugs of beer and a basket of hush puppies.

Griffin picked up a hush puppy from the paper-lined basket, stared at the deep-fried blob of cornmeal for a long moment, then put it back where he got it. "My wife died of yellow fever," he said bluntly, his gaze fixed on the plastic basket.

His words hit Meredith like a bolt from the blue, causing her heart to skip a beat. "Your—your wife?" Meredith asked, attempting to eliminate the shock from her voice.

"Jane," he said without emotion. "She died four years ago . . . with our son. There was an outbreak of yellow fever all along the James."

"Did you catch it?"

He laughed, the sound bitter with self-disgust. "I was not there. I was at sea, on my way back from London, captaining the *Spirit*. I was so pleased with myself. I had a hold full of China tea I'd traded for Virginia tobacco. And I had purchased a cradle with a bit of our profits. When I arrived in Williamsburg, my father was waiting at the dock. He told me Jane had given me a son. Then he told me they had both succumbed to the fever, just three days apart."

"I'm sorry," Meredith said softly. "You must have loved her very much."

He shook his head. "When we married, I barely knew her. But we came to care about each other. She was a good woman. Whenever I would leave for another long voyage, she would smile and kiss me goodbye. She never complained. She gave me a son. I will not soon forget that."

"Life is a very fragile thing where you come from," Meredith said.

His jaw tightened. "Do you know how they fight the fever in my time? They fire cannons and muskets, and people carry bits of tar with them. They soak sponges in camphor and dip handkerchiefs in vinegar. And they put garlic in their shoes. I am not a physician, Merrie, but even I sense this is not right. Yet I have no idea what might prevent this disease."

"You should drain stagnant ponds and dump out every barrel of rainwater. The fever is spread by mosquitoes."

He looked at her in shock. "Mosquitoes?" He considered the notion for a moment, then tipped his head back and sighed. "I find it a great irony that I've come to a time where women and children do not die of the fever, where a prick of a needle can protect a life against a tiny insect and Jane needn't have died." He paused and shook his head. "A great irony."

"There are many diseases which we've found cures for—typhus, smallpox, measles, the plague. But there are others that still baffle medical science. I guess things haven't changed that much."

They sat in silence for a long while. Meredith was startled by the traces of agony that etched his frozen expression. Slowly, she reached out and wove her fingers through his. "Thank you for telling me," she said. "It helps me to understand."

He didn't reply, merely stared out at the harbor, his features frozen. Meredith's heart ached for him, for his dead wife and the baby son he'd never held. For she could see in the depths of his pale eyes that he blamed himself for their deaths. And she could see that the blame was eating away at him.

And in that instant, she knew it was not just his honor standing between them, but his guilt.

THE LATE-AFTERNOON SUN beat down on Griffin's bare back as he scraped another layer of paint off the hull of the old shrimp boat. It felt good to labor again, to work so hard the sweat dripped from his forehead and his muscles ached.

He'd been working for nearly a week and he and Merrie had slipped into an easy routine, a routine in which they kept a careful but friendly distance from each other. Still, the attraction between them had not diminished, and though he only visited her bedroom while she slept, he had been hard-pressed to keep from touching her in all the ways he wanted to.

The thought of her body beneath his hands caused a flood of warmth to pool in his lap and he quickly turned back to work, scraping at the paint with renewed vigor.

Early Jackson was below deck, tinkering with the engine, leaving Griffin to his own thoughts. From the time Griffin was a child, he'd been fascinated by boats and ships. He and his father had spent hours together, carving model-ship hulls from wood before they commissioned the *Betty*. And at one time, Griffin had thought he might prefer the building of ships to the sailing of them.

In his year at William and Mary, he'd studied mathematics to better understand the design of a hull and the efficiency of a sail. Now, as he worked on refurbishing the shrimper, he found a certain satisfaction in bringing a battered old boat back to life.

Perhaps this would not be a bad way to make a living. Surely there were many boats like this one, boats that needed a tender hand and a loving eye. Griffin stood and stretched, examining the morning's work.

If the boat were his, instead of Early's, he would treat her with much more care. He would strip her to the bare wood and sand her until she was smooth as silk. Then he would lay on a perfect coat of white paint. And after every piece of brightwork was varnished and every winch spit-shined, he would hand-carve a nameplate for each side of the bow. Griffin smiled to himself. And he'd call her the *Merry Girl*.

"Hey, sailor. How about some supper?"

Griffin shaded his eyes against the sun and found Merrie watching him from the side of the road, a teasing smile on her face. She was wearing a loose cotton dress in cornflower blue, which left her arms bare, and a pair of sandals that allowed her toes to peek out. He still hadn't gotten used to seeing Merrie's feet and ankles displayed in public, much less her knees, but that didn't prevent him from appreciating the view.

Bracing his shoulder on the boat's cradle, he grinned and waved.

She jogged up to the boat, swinging a basket at her side. "Are you hungry?" she asked.

"Ravenous," he said. He pulled up the cloth that covered the contents of the basket and peered inside. "Did you bring me a soda pop?"

She pulled out a can and flipped the top. "What are you going to do when you go back and you can't have soda pop with every meal?"

He wiped his hands on the ragged, paint-spattered blue jeans that Early had given him, then took a long swallow of the cold pop, nearly draining the can. "Maybe I will just have to stay," he said. "The prospect of life without soda pop is nearly too much to bear."

She laughed, taking his words more lightly than they were really meant. By the minute, the prospect of life without Merrie was becoming even more unthinkable. He looked forward to seeing her every day, to listening to her musical voice, to watching her face light up with a smile.

"Can you take some time to eat? We can have supper right here if you like."

He slipped into his shirt, then grabbed her hand. "I have a better idea. I am finished for the day. Come." Griffin snatched the basket from her hands and dragged her across the parking lot, then stopped beside a small motorcycle. "We will go for a ride."

Merrie stared at the motorcycle. "I don't know how to drive this thing."

"Ah, but I do. Early taught me a few days ago. He sends me down to the hardware store on this machine to fetch supplies. 'Tis quite . . . exhilarating."

"You can't drive this without a license," Merrie said.

Griffin frowned. "What is a license? Early did not tell me this."

"It's a permit that allows you to drive on the roads. Didn't you tell Early you don't have a driver's license?"

Griffin shrugged. "How could I tell him this if I didn't know I needed one?" He climbed onto the bike and pushed it back off its stand. "Get on. We'll go for a ride now."

"I don't think so," Merrie said.

"Come," he said, grabbing her hand. "We'll have fun. And I will not drive fast."

With a reluctant smile, Merrie climbed onto the back of the bike. Griffin wedged the basket between them, then kicked the starter as Early had taught him. Moments later, they were weaving down the narrow road that circled the harbor. When they reached the highway, Griffin turned and headed out of town.

As he promised, he didn't drive fast, but Merrie still clutched his waist with both hands. "I can't believe I'm doing this!" she shouted.

He laughed, then twisted the throttle, increasing the bike's speed. She screamed and grabbed him more tightly as they sped down the highway. Once they left the boundaries of the village, all signs of civilization disappeared, save for the long strip of paved road in front of them.

Most of the island was a national seashore, he had been told, though he wasn't sure exactly what that meant. What he did know was there were no houses or people beyond the town. The island looked much as it had when he'd first sailed past it nearly three centuries ago—sweeping sand dunes, pristine beaches and tall sea grass waving in the breeze.

Griffin turned off the main road and followed a sandy path, then stopped the motorcycle. Merrie slipped off the back and ran her fingers through her windblown hair still clutching the basket with one white-knuckled hand. He climbed off the bike and stood beside her. "'Tis like riding a very fast horse," he said.

"I've never ridden a horse, so I wouldn't know," Merrie replied.

"Trust me, this is much better. Come, we will have a picnic on the beach. I want to relax. I have worked hard today."

Hand in hand, they climbed up one side of a dune and slid down the other. In front of them, the deserted white sand beach stretched long and wide. Waves broke against the shore, and above the brilliant blue water, seabirds dipped and swayed on the breeze.

Griffin grabbed the small tablecloth from the basket and spread it out on the sand, then pulled Merrie down beside him. As she unpacked the basket, he watched her, enjoying the sight of her bright eyes and rosy cheeks and quick smile.

Over the past week, they had spent little time together. Griffin had worked from sunrise to sunset, glad for a reason to put some distance between himself and Merrie. It had become much more difficult of late to see her and ignore the deep stirring of desire she provoked in him.

Most nights, he fell asleep on the couch after dinner. Hours later, in the middle of the night, as he paced the floors of the cottage, he would sneak into her bedroom and watch her sleep, always certain to leave before dawn without waking her. If she knew he was there, she didn't speak of it in the light of day. In fact, she seemed to prefer this space between them, as if it made living together, and the prospect of his leaving, much easier.

He was beginning to wonder if he'd ever go back. Every night he stood on the beach at midnight, waiting for some sign, for the powers that had brought him here to snatch him up and send him back. But night after night, nothing happened. He was running out of time and there was nothing he could do about it.

Griffin rested his arms on his bent knees and stared out at the ocean. He pointed to the east. "See that?" he asked.

Merrie squinted into the distance. "What?"

He leaned nearer to her, his shoulder brushing hers. To his relief, she didn't move away, but tipped her head closer. "There," he murmured, turning to inhale the fresh scent of her hair. His gaze drifted along the delicate features of her face and came to rest on her perfect mouth. He'd nearly forgotten how she could addle his brain with just a guileless smile. "Just beyond the horizon."

She squinted. "I don't see anything."

"England," he said. "'Tis right over there ... somewhere."

Merrie turned to look at him, then blinked in surprise at his sudden nearness. "If that's how you navigate," she said softly, "remind me never to get on a boat with you again." With trembling hands, she dug through the basket, then pushed a sandwich at him.

Griffin unwrapped the sandwich and took a bite, glad for a brief distraction. "I believe I would like to see London in your time," he said as he chewed. "It must be a grand city by now."

"It is," Merrie said, her expression uneasy.

"Then you have been there?"

"Several times. But I would like to see London in *your* time, before cars and buses and modern buildings."

"Then I will send you back to deal with Blackbeard," he said. "There are times when I swear you could charm the man into surrender with just a simple smile."

Merrie gave him a sideways glance. "They say he was quite the ladies' man."

"He is said to have married many women," Griffin replied. "Most put the number at ten or twelve, but no one is certain." He paused. "Early Jackson was telling me a story about a pirate festival Teach held on the island in late September 1718. According to him, 'tis quite a colorful legend. The afternoon I went overboard, Teach was planning to set sail for Ocracoke. Do you know of this legend?"

Merrie nodded hesitantly.

"Then tell me of it. I want to know it, everything."

"I—I don't know much," she began, "but they anchored their ships in Teach's Hole and went ashore on the southern tip of the island. Charles Vane was there, and Calico Jack Rackham, and Robert Deal and Israel Hands. They barbecued a couple cows and hogs, and drank a lot of rum. There was music and dancing. When word of this festival reached Governor Spotswood, the story had become twisted into the news that the pirates were building a fortress on the island. It was after this that he began to make firm plans to set off for Ocracoke and capture Blackbeard."

"You know much about this legend," Griffin said.

"Everyone knows about it," Merrie replied, a hint of defensiveness in her voice. "Not just me."

He frowned. "I have been thinking. Perhaps there is no reason for me to go back," he said. "Perhaps it will all happen without me."

"You can't know that," Merrie said. "Not for sure. You have the journal and the letters. For all we know, those may have had an effect on Spotswood's decision, or on the outcome."

He turned to face her. "But I am beginning to think there *is* no way back, Merrie. We have tried everything, to no avail."

She gave him a sideways glance. "Would that be so bad, if you couldn't return?" Her green eyes were filled with curiosity.

He stared at her for a moment, then, with a frustrated sigh, he lay back on the sand and threw his arm over his eyes. "I have invested so much of my energy over the past year on bringing Blackbeard down," he murmured. "It has become part of who I am. I would like to think that I might have had the chance to put a finish to this, to make Teach pay for what he did to my father."

"And maybe you still will," she said.

Griffin laughed harshly. "Damn, I do not even know how I got here!" He pulled his arm from his eyes and found Merrie leaning over him.

"Griffin, there is something . . . something I need to tell you."

"What is it?"

She bit her bottom lip and winced. "You'll be angry."

He reached out and cupped her cheek in his palm. "What troubles you so, Merrie?"

"It's just that I—I—" Suddenly, without warning, she brought her mouth down on his and kissed him, quick and hard. Then, as if she'd surprised even herself, she drew away, her eyes wide with shock.

Gently, Griffin placed his hand on her nape and drew her closer. "I cannot be happy with just one sweet taste, Merrie-girl," he murmured against her lips. "I must have more."

She opened to him and he pressed her mouth to his, quietly demanding her surrender. Hesitantly, her tongue touched his and a warm rush of desire washed over him, heating his blood, making his pulse race. Lord, how could he fight this, these exquisite sensations that her touch aroused?

Wrapping his arms around her waist, he pulled her beneath him, settling himself against her bewitching body, his hips pressed against hers. How long had it been since he'd felt such need for a woman? He'd lost himself in so many after Jane's death, and though they'd slaked the ache in his loins, none had soothed the ache he felt deep in his heart. After a time, he'd stopped trying to numb the pain and avoided women altogether.

But somehow, he knew Merrie would make his heart soar with pleasure and his body shudder with passion. He would bury himself deep inside her and there he would find his release. The past would finally melt away and he would be left with only the present...and the future...and the woman who had freed him from his demons.

Without breaking their kiss, he pushed up on one arm and reached between them, fumbling with the buttons of her dress. One by one, he loosened them, then relinquished her lips for the silken skin of her neck and shoulder. He parted the bodice of her dress and slipped his palm inside, then froze.

Instinct had trained him to expect another layer or two, a chemise and a corset at least. Instead, his hand cupped the soft flesh of her breast and hard bud of her nipple. He sucked in a sharp breath and held it, waiting until the overwhelming need for release passed.

He had thought to deny this attraction between them would be to honor her. But now he knew he was wrong, for to make love to her, to give himself entirely to this woman, without reserve, would be the greatest honor of all.

Griffin brushed his lips along her collarbone, tasting her silken skin and tracing a path between her breasts. And then, with exquisite care, he drew her nipple softly between his lips, teasing at it with his teeth, exciting it with his tongue.

She moaned softly, then whispered his name. Weaving her fingers through his hair, she pressed him against her, the sweet torment of his mouth on her breast no longer enough for her.

Griffin focused his thoughts, trying to control his hunger. He knew the moment he entered her, he would be lost in an explosion of long-denied need. So he would take her slowly, treating her with great care and bringing her own passions to the surface, waiting until she was ready for him at last.

Reaching down, he drew her leg up against his thigh, sliding his palm along the length of her limb, his hard shaft fitted against a spot between her thighs. "I need you, Merrie," he murmured. He drew back and pressed his palm against her cheek, stroking her reddened lips with his thumb. "Faith, but I think I must have been brought here to make love to you, for there is no other reason I can fathom."

Her eyes snapped open and she looked directly at him, her expression suddenly lucid, the hazy passion in her eyes clearing like the morning fog beneath the sun.

"I—I can't do this," she murmured. She glanced around, then wiggled out from under him, clutching at the buttons of her dress. "I—I'm sorry...I shouldn't have...I mean, this was all my fault."

"Merrie, wait. I did not mean to—"

"We should go now." She grabbed the basket and stumbled to her feet. "I—I'll meet you back at the road." Griffin watched as she clambered up the dune, slipping and sliding against the steep mound of sand. When she disappeared behind it, he flopped back down and cursed out loud.

What the devil had he done wrong? He knew things between men and women had changed in the past three centuries. But a woman's honor was now her own responsibility—or so Merrie had told him. Besides, she'd had other men and how many, he didn't care to speculate. Had he been so inept that he hadn't even lived up to her past lovers? No, that couldn't be so! She had responded to his touch, urging him on with her soft, pleading moans.

Griffin groaned. For the first time in a very long while, he felt like a fumbling boy, untrained in the ways of the world. He had made a mess of things, of that he was certain.

There was only one solution to his dilemma, to this war that raged between his past and his present. He had little chance of returning to his own time. No matter how much he wanted to go back, he'd have to come to terms with making a life here, in the twentieth century. So he would do the only proper thing after their unfortunate encounter on the beach. All their problems would be solved.

He would simply take Merrie as his wife.

THE NIGHT BREEZE BLEW softly through the screened porch, ruffling Meredith's hair and cooling her flushed skin. Curling her feet beneath her on the chaise longue, she listened idly to the songs of the crickets and the gentle ebb and flow of the waves. But her eyes never strayed from the figure that stood on the beach, illuminated by the light of a half moon.

Griffin stood at the water's edge, staring out across the Sound, his hands braced on his hips. He'd been there since they'd arrived back home, pacing, then stopping to gaze at the horizon. He'd spent many midnights in the same spot, watching and waiting, at the edge of the water while she pretended to sleep. But tonight was different.

He was still dressed in the faded jeans and ragged shirt that he'd worn to work. The leather pouch was still sitting on the mantel and his boots and breeches were inside the hall closet. For the first time in many nights, Griffin was not waiting to leave. And in that realization, Meredith knew she should feel some joy. But all she felt was utter confusion and a healthy dose of remorse.

She drew a long breath and closed her eyes. She'd wanted to go to him, to explain her sudden rejection of his advances, but then she'd thought better of it. For an explanation would also require a confession, and she wasn't sure he was ready to listen to what she had to say. Nor was she prepared to tell him what she'd been trying to deny from the night he'd arrived...that *she* was the cause of his leap in time.

Meredith covered her eyes with her hands. It had to be the truth, nothing else made sense. Over the past week, she'd carefully questioned him about Blackbeard, knowing full well it may be the catalyst to send him back. But to her surprise, she'd discovered that Griffin knew very little about the man he hunted and could provide few facts that she didn't already know. She'd somehow forgotten that news did not travel fast in colonial America. Without the benefit of newspapers and television, news of Blackbeard's crimes and background had been spread mostly by word of mouth.

She was now certain she'd brought him here as an answer to her fantasies. Over the past week, she had desperately tried to a recall a specific incident, an errant musing or a frustrated thought that may have provided the key. Yet nothing had come to mind. One day she was happily writing a biography and the next night, he was lying on her beach, half dead, her fantasy man come to life.

She would have to tell him the truth before their relationship went any further. But she couldn't bring herself to say the words without sounding as if she'd lost her mind.

Meredith snatched her hands from her eyes. "What am I supposed to do?" she muttered to herself.

"Perhaps you could begin by explaining what happened between us, Merrie."

She sat upright, her gaze riveted on Griffin who was standing at the end the chaise. Damn his pirate tricks! He moved like a cat, with unerring stealth. So much for her plan to be safely locked in her bedroom before he headed back inside.

"I—I really don't know what to say," Meredith said.

"Did I do something wrong?"

Meredith got to her feet. "Oh, no," she said nervously. "It's my fault. I guess—I guess I just wasn't ready. There are some things that we need to talk about before we...you know."

"'Tis my fault," Griffin countered. "I pushed you."

"No...no, you didn't." Meredith winced. "Griffin, I think you should know that I'm the one who is—"

Griffin reached out and placed his finger over her lips. "Merrie, I think I know what you want to say."

"Griffin, I—"

"As I see it, there is only one solution to this problem between us. We must marry."

Meredith looked up and met his gaze, then shook her head in confusion. "What?"

"I want you to be my wife."

"You—you want me to *marry* you?"

He nodded. "After this afternoon, I believe it is the only honorable thing to do. My behavior was improper and ill-mannered. And though I know you do not have a care for your virtue, I must."

"And you think *you'll* protect *my* virtue by marrying me?" Meredith asked, unable to contain her disbelief. "Are you crazy?"

Griffin shifted on his feet and frowned, obviously not getting the response he'd expected. "No, I am in complete control of my faculties."

Meredith laughed. "You want to marry me because of one little roll in the sand? We didn't do anything!"

"We did plenty. Now, will you marry me or not?"

"No!" Meredith shouted. For an instant, she couldn't believe she was actually turning down his marriage proposal. But then, she knew she had no other choice.

Griffin took a step back. "I don't understand. Why not?"

"What about when you go back? Do you really expect me to marry someone who might suddenly get yanked back to his own century? Just so you won't feel guilty when we sleep together?"

Griffin grabbed her hands. "Merrie, let us be honest here. I don't think I will be going back. With every day that passes, this fact becomes more real to me."

"You—you can't be sure of that," she said.

"Marry me," he repeated.

"No," Meredith said, snatching her hands from his. "I will not marry you, Griffin Rourke."

With that, she turned and walked through the door, making a point to slam it behind her. Of all the nerve! Who did he think he was? She couldn't imagine a more ridiculous proposal. Honor? He could take his half-witted proposal and his moral obligation and shove it, for all she cared.

"Damn it, Merrie, wait!"

"Leave me alone, Griffin!"

Meredith strode to her bedroom and slammed that door, as well. "A marriage proposal should be based on love, not some debt of honor," she muttered. "If he thinks

I'd even consider such an insult, he's more provincial than I thought!"

Meredith threw herself on the bed and covered her head with a pillow. All right, so maybe she was tempted to accept. Deep inside, she wanted nothing more than to spend her life with Griffin Rourke. But she also wanted a marriage based on love, not duty. And she was not fool enough to believe that Griffin loved her. He may desire her, but he did not love her. In his mind, love was not necessary to make a good marriage.

Yet, that didn't stop her from wanting him. There wasn't a minute that passed in which she didn't think of him and didn't wonder what it might be like between them. And the more time that passed, the more she began to see him as a man who belonged in her time.

When he was dressed in body-hugging jeans and a torn T-shirt, she could almost believe that he had been born in the same decade as she had. His speech had even slipped into more familiar patterns and as time passed, he seemed more comfortable with his surroundings.

Meredith sighed. Who was she trying to fool? When it came right down to it, he was still Griffin Rourke—a man whose heart and soul belonged to the past.

7

MEREDITH THOUGHT Griffin might come to her bed that night, but he didn't. She woke at least once to hear him pacing outside her bedroom door. Several times he stopped and she could imagine his hand gripping the knob. She slowed her breathing and pretended to sleep, but he didn't venture inside. Finally, the house had grown silent and she'd drifted off into a dreamless slumber.

When she awoke, it was well past dawn. From the living room, she could hear Ben Gunn carrying on a one-sided conversation from his perch next to her desk. Meredith rolled out of bed and stretched, grateful that Griffin had already left for work and relieved that she wouldn't have to face him.

The last thing she wanted to discuss was his marriage proposal. She knew her refusal had stung his considerable pride, but there was much more to be solved between them before they could consider a future together. If he truly was here to stay, then she would have time . . . time to make him love her—before she told him why she really believed he'd come to her.

She pulled on a pair of jeans and a T-shirt, then padded to the kitchen to put on a pot of coffee.

"Morning!" Ben cried, adding a wolf whistle to his cheerful greeting.

"Good morn—"

Meredith cut short her reply to the gray parrot. She and the bird were not alone. Griffin stood in front of the fireplace, staring into an empty grate, his arms braced on the mantel, the muscles of his back tense beneath the soft fabric of his paint-spattered T-shirt. Her gaze drifted to the tight contours of his backside. The man was meant for denim, she mused.

Griffin slowly turned to face her. Her hesitant smile faded when it met a mask of cold indifference. He stared at her for a long moment. When he didn't speak, she did.

"It's late. Why aren't you at work?" she asked, watching him warily.

Her words seemed to crack his icy facade and he raised a dark eyebrow. "When did you plan to tell me, Merrie?"

Meredith ran her fingers through her hair. "What are you talking about? Tell you what?"

He reached over and picked up a stack of papers from her desk, then held them out to her. "About this," he said, waving them at her. "Your work. The subject of the book you're writing."

Meredith's breath caught in her throat. "You searched my desk?"

He let out a laugh, a harsh sound without a trace of humor. "Of course I searched your desk. You forget, Merrie, I'm a spy. If I need information, I make it my business to find it."

"You had no right," Meredith said softly.

"No right!" Ben mimicked.

Griffin glared at the bird, then leveled a cool gaze on her. "I had no right? I had every right," he said, his voice deceptively even. "When, Merrie? How long did you expect to keep this from me?"

She stepped back, surprised at the intensity of his tightly leashed anger, and unable to answer. How long? She had never *wanted* to keep it from him, there had just never

seemed to be a good time to tell him. And then, later, it
didn't make any difference.

"Tell me now," Griffin demanded. "Tell me that you
have spent years studying the man I despise, that you plan
to write a book glorifying his crimes. Tell me that you
would do anything to learn more about Teach. Tell me that
you are the reason I am here. For 'tis the only thing that
makes sense," he said. "*You* brought me here, Merrie.
Now, tell me how you did it!"

"I don't know!" she cried. "I've searched my brain since
the night you arrived, but I can't recall anything that
would have prompted you to land here. But you're not here
because of my work, that much I do know."

"If not your work, then what?"

"I—I can't tell you," she said. "It's just so crazy, even I
don't believe it."

"Damn it, Merrie, I have a right to know exactly how
and why you've manipulated my life."

She drew a deep breath. "You're my fantasy man," she
said, the words coming out in a rush.

He gasped. "What?"

Meredith felt a blush creep up her cheeks and warm her
skin. "I—I've had these dreams, these . . . sexual fantasies
about a pirate. But they were just fantasies," she cried. "I
didn't mean any harm. I didn't mean to bring you here, I
swear it."

Griffin laughed harshly. "I have been in your world long
enough to know that many strange and unfathomable
things are possible, but this I do not believe. I was not
brought here to take you to bed! I would not have been
taken from my task simply to satisfy some woman's erotic
fantasies."

"Then why?" she challenged. "Nothing else makes
sense. I know more about Teach than you do. Nothing

you've told me is new. At first I was afraid to talk to you about Blackbeard for fear you might be snatched back into your own time. Kelsey warned me that to do so might alter history in some way."

"You've already altered history," he said. "You brought me here, and took me from my task."

Meredith rubbed at the growing knot of tension in her temple. "If I was the cause of your coming here, I'm sorry. And if I could undo it, I would."

"Then there has to be more," he muttered. "We have missed something. *You* have missed something." His voice was cold and accusatory.

"If I knew how to send you back, don't you think I would?"

"I don't know, Merrie. Would you?"

"How can you even think that?" she asked.

He cursed beneath his breath. "What, then? I am just left to live out my life in this time and place."

She threw up her hands in frustration. "You make it sound so appealing," she said. "Do you find life here that objectionable?"

"I *had* a life, in my *own* century," Griffin said, punctuating his words with a jab to his chest. "It is not so simple to forget that."

She scoffed. "A life? You had an all-consuming plan for revenge. Is that what you call a life?" Meredith demanded.

Her aim was true and her volley hit its mark. Griffin cursed, then turned away, bracing his hands on the mantel again. She could feel his anger all the way across the room, could see it in his tightly coiled body, could hear it in his harsh breathing.

"Is this plan for revenge that important to you?" she asked, wanting to reach out and touch him, to soothe his anger. "If so, why didn't you kill Teach when you had the chance, on his ship, while he slept?"

He refused to face her. "To murder him would make me no better than the criminal he is. Teach was responsible for my father's death. I will be sure he pays for his crime."

"Tell me about that," she said. "I mean, if you've been brought here for my research then why don't we take advantage of it while we can. *My* research says that Blackbeard was not a bloodthirsty murderer. Though I have read of his capture of the *Betty,* I have yet to find a record of him killing a man named Rourke."

Griffin turned, his eyes hard with anger. "He did not kill him by his hand," he said. "Teach killed him by his deeds."

"And what does that mean? Explain it to me. Make me understand."

Griffin's expression softened slightly and he drew a deep, steadying breath. "When Teach attacked the *Betty,* he put everyone on board ashore. My father watched as the pirates scuttled the ship and it sank off Cape Charles. When he returned home, my father wasn't . . . right. Over the next several months, he grew very sad and quiet, the same as when he lost my mother. The doctors came and bled him, doused him with calomel, but it did no good. He died soon after."

Meredith's heart twisted in her chest. "Calomel? Are you sure of this?"

"Yes. What of it?"

She winced, then bit her bottom lip. Oh, Lord, she'd have to tell him. He needed to know. She drew a shaky breath. "Griffin, no matter how much you want to, you cannot blame your father's death on Teach." Her voice filled with sympathy for him, for she knew what she was about to say would hurt him deeply.

"My father was a fine and healthy man until he ran afoul of the devil."

Meredith slowly crossed the room and took his hand in hers. He stiffened at her touch. "Your father became ill *after* this incident. And maybe his condition was brought on by his upsetting experience with Blackbeard," she said softly. "Or maybe he wasn't even sick, but simply depressed. The fact is, the medicine the doctors administered probably killed your father."

"No," Griffin said, shaking his head, suspicion clouding his blue eyes. "That cannot be so. They were the best physicians in Williamsburg. I made certain of that."

She squeezed his hand. "Calomel was made with mercury chloride. And mercury chloride is poisonous. George Washington, the first president of the United States, died from the effects of the same treatments your father probably received."

"Are—are you saying it was *my* fault?"

"Of course not," she cried. "You did what you thought was best for your father. You can't be blamed for the state of medicine at that time. I'm just saying that you might want to rethink your determination to bring down Blackbeard."

"Rethink?" Griffin asked, snatching his hand from hers. "What does that mean? That you don't agree with what I'm trying to do? The man is evil incarnate, Merrie, and someone has to put an end to his plague of piracy."

She clutched his arm. "I believe Teach needs to be stopped, too. But I don't believe *you're* the one to do it."

"And why is that? Because your history books tell a different story? Or because it soothes your conscience to think as much?"

She sighed and shook her head. "Consider for a moment that you were brought here for another reason."

"What might that be?"

"Maybe you were brought here for your own good. To protect you." She stalked over to the desk and pulled a file folder off a tall stack, then snatched a paper from inside. "Here," she said, holding it out to him. "This is a copy of a letter to the British Admiralty. It relates that at the end of the battle with Teach, Lieutenant Robert Maynard's men advanced on the few members of Blackbeard's crew who had retreated onto the pirate ship. During this time, one of Maynard's men was shot and killed by another member of the Royal Navy, when the man was mistaken for one of the pirates."

Griffin leaned back against the mantel and crossed his arms over his chest. "And what does this have to do with me?"

"That man could *be* you!" Meredith cried. "I've searched all my sources, but can find no reference to this man's name. If he were an official member of Maynard's crew, he would have been listed by name, but he's not. And he was mistaken for a pirate. You *were* a pirate on Teach's ship."

He shrugged. "But then, it may not be me," Griffin said. "How can you be sure?"

Meredith cursed beneath her breath and balled her fists at her side. "What more proof do you need? You were sent here to save your fool life!" she cried.

"I don't need anyone to *save* me," he countered. "Especially not you."

"Why, because I'm a woman? Because your stubborn male pride would not allow it?"

Griffin pushed off the mantel. "Because I can take care of my own affairs," he replied evenly, an arrogant glint in his eyes. "And I would not burden anyone else, not even you, with my problems."

"And damn anyone who cares about you, is that it?" Meredith said.

"That is not what I meant," he replied. "The habit of putting words into my mouth does not become you, Merrie."

"How can I help it?" she said. "You never explain yourself, so I'm left to do it for you."

"I do not need to explain myself to you or anyone else."

Meredith shook her head. "Just because you allow yourself to need someone, to heed someone else's advice, doesn't mean you're weak. It means you're human." She paused, then asked him the question she knew would decide their future together. "Tell me the truth, Griffin. If you could go back, right this instant, would you?"

He closed his eyes and tipped his head back. The silence hung between them. Finally, he took a deep breath and spoke, gazing directly into her eyes. "Yes," he said. "I would."

Meredith laughed bitterly. "Then I guess I was right not to take your marriage proposal too seriously."

Griffin stalked across the room and grabbed her upper arms. "That has nothing at all to do with my desire to go back and finish what I began. Just because I *want* to return, does not mean that I *expect* to return."

"So I am merely part of your contingency plan?"

"Damn it, Merrie, you test my patience!" he snapped, giving her a gentle shake. "And you put words in my mouth again. What do you want me to tell you? You ask for the truth, but when I speak it, you don't like what you hear. I care for you, more than I've ever cared about a woman in my life. Is that not enough?"

"Then why do you want to go back?"

He loosened his grip, then rubbed her arms with his palms. "I would not be a man if I did not finish this fight with Teach. These are two different issues, you and Teach. How can you speak of them as if they are one?"

She shook her head. "If you don't know, then we have nothing more to discuss," she said in a quiet voice.

Griffin raked his hands through his hair. "On this one point, I will concede you may be right," he said. "We will speak of this no longer. I must get to work." He strode toward the door.

"We will speak of this *again*," she corrected. "We'll continue this discussion when you get home."

He froze for an instant, his hand on the knob. But then he shook his head, opened the door and pulled it closed behind him.

"Stubborn fool," Meredith muttered.

"Stubborn fool, stubborn fool," Ben repeated.

GRIFFIN STRODE through the chill morning air, his breath visible in icy puffs in front of his face. But he barely noticed the cold, so intent was he on his thoughts.

"Stubborn wench," he muttered. "I vow, I have never met a woman like her!"

Always, she had an opinion, and always, she believed *she* was right! What had happened to the fair sex over the past three centuries? The women in his world were quiet, complacent, always happy to defer to a man's greater experience and authority. *This* was what he'd been brought up to believe was the paragon of womanhood.

"Instead, I am forced to live with an acid-tongued virago who insists on knowing my every thought and feeling," he added. And to make matters worse, after he'd been forced to reveal himself, she wanted to discuss it all at great and detailed length! Was he to keep nothing to himself in this world of hers?

But the worst was not her prying, but her meddling in his life. A man was supposed to make the decisions where his own life was concerned. She acted as if she had a say in the choices he made and the course he set for himself.

Jane had not expected—Griffin stopped himself. Merrie was not Jane and to compare the two would be unfair to both. Merrie was a woman living in a world so changed from his, it was barely recognizable. How could she help but be different from Jane? He cursed himself roundly. And how could he blame her for simply being herself? And for caring about him?

He should be happy that someone did care. After all, he had no one left in this world, not a single person who gave a damn whether he lived or died. But she cared. She showed it in every little thing she did for him, every kind gesture and sweet smile and gentle touch.

Truth be told, he loved her exactly the way she was. Merrie would not be Merrie with a timid smile and a yielding nature. He loved her fire and her passion and her inquisitive spirit. He loved her intelligence and quick wit. He loved . . .

Griffin stopped at the side of the road and frowned. Damn, was that it? Did he *love* her? He groaned, then cursed softly. No, he wouldn't allow himself such foolishness. But then . . .

Perhaps he did love her. Yet how could he be certain of his feelings? He'd never been in love before. In fact, he had never even considered the notion. Love was meant for sentimental poets and blushing virgins.

But his feelings for Merrie ran as deep and as strong as an ocean current, drawing him toward her against all will. It mattered not that he steered away from her, her pull was ever present and impossible to fight.

Then why was he still determined to return to his own time? Was it because of Teach? Or was it because he couldn't bear to open his life to another woman, to risk the pain that it might cause? He had cared deeply about Jane and it had nearly killed him when he lost her. He couldn't imagine living if he ever lost Merrie.

Perhaps that was part of it. But there was more...much more. Here, in her world, he felt as if he was incomplete in some way. As if part of his being had been left behind in his own time. Teach was waiting for him. But to be honest, the pirate was not the objective, but simply a means to an end. A way to finally say goodbye to his father.

With Jane and the baby, there had been a reason for their deaths, a reason he couldn't fight. But with his father, he'd just watched him fade before his very eyes, unable to understand why he had chosen to abandon his life and unable to do anything to bring him back. To destroy Teach might somehow give meaning to his father's death.

How could he explain this to Merrie in a way that she would understand? She would never comprehend the sense of family duty his father had instilled in him, the strong moral fiber and uncompromising honor by which he lived his life. These were things a man did not speak of, for they were the fabric of his very soul.

No, these things were not meant to be said aloud. Griffin picked up his pace until he was nearly running. She would never understand.

The harbor was already bustling with activity when he arrived at Early Jackson's dock. The shrimp boat sat in its cradle at the edge of the water, the hull nearly scraped bare. He circled the boat, admiring the practical lines and sturdy construction. The shrimper had been built by hand, the same way boats of his time had. He knocked his fist on the hull and listened to the solid, dependable sound.

"Morning, Griff."

Griffin glanced up to see Early Jackson ten feet above him, hanging over the side of the boat with a bucket in his hand. He smiled. "Morning, Early. I didn't see you up there."

The spritely old man crawled over the side and scrambled down the ladder. "You're a little slow getting in this morning."

Griffin shrugged. "Sorry. I'll work later tonight."

"Naw, I don't care if you take some time for yourself. You've been working so hard these past few days, I'm sure Meredith would like to keep you at home a little longer."

Griffin nodded and peered inside the bucket, then pulled out his favorite scraper. Without a word, he set to work, scraping the wood with strong, sure strokes. Early watched him with a bemused expression.

"Is everything all right between you and Meredith?" he asked.

"Why do you ask?" Griffin replied.

"Because, if you scrape much harder, you're going to scrape a hole right through the hull. You might feel better if you talk about it."

Griffin stood up. Why was every facet of his personal life open for discussion in this century? He braced his fists on his hips, ready to tell Early it was none of his business. But then he thought better of it, and replaced his retort with a question. "Are you married, Early?"

The old man rubbed his whiskered chin. "Yep. Nearly forty years . . . and to the same gal, I might add."

"May I pose a question to you?"

Early shrugged. "Sure. Pose away."

"Who has the last word in your household? You or your wife?"

"She does," Early said without a moment's thought.

Griffin frowned, certain that he had not made himself clear. "What I mean to ask is, who is in command?"

"She is," Early said.

Griffin cleared his throat. "I don't believe you understand my question. Let me restate it. Do you consider her opinion in all that you do?"

Early snorted, then chuckled. "Are you crazy?"

He smiled, relieved that he'd finally gotten the answer he wanted. Things were not so different here.

"Of course I do," Early continued. "I'm no fool, boy."

Griffin opened his mouth, then snapped it shut, considering Early's answer for a moment. "This is common then," he finally asked, "this bowing to your wife's will?"

"Me and Millie just figured that marriage should be an equal partnership. I give a little, she gives a little. It keeps things interesting and on a nice even keel."

"An *equal* partnership?"

"When we got married, most folks didn't think that way. But Millie made it clear she wouldn't marry me unless I respected her as an individual. Then came the women's movement, and now everybody pretty much thinks this way. I like to tell Millie we were ahead of our time."

"And this does not bother you...to give up control? Isn't it a bit like a ship with two captains?"

"I never really wanted control in the first place," Early said with a chuckle. "Not since I figured out that I loved the lady. After that, it didn't much matter. Besides, we usually take turns at the wheel, one of us steering while the other navigates. It makes the trip easier for the both of us." Early paused, then slapped Griffin on the shoulder. "Don't worry. You'll work it out. Meredith can be as stubborn as a cross-eyed mule. She gets that from her daddy. But she's got a good heart, something her mama had in spades."

"Yes," Griffin said quietly, "that she does." He smiled. "That she does."

"Now, seeing as how you're going to make up with Meredith, I suspect you'll be staying on the island for a while longer. I was wondering if you might want some more work. Me and the boys found two more shrimpers, but we don't have time to work on them both. We figured we'd give one to you to fix up. When we sell it, we'll split the profits right down the middle. Does that sound good?"

Griffin hesitated before he answered. To agree would be to admit that he would spend the rest of his life in this time and place. Was he really ready to do that, to give up on the past and go on with his future? "That sounds fair," he finally replied. "But I'd like to have a few days to consider your proposal, if you don't mind."

"I'm sure you'd like to discuss it with Meredith," Early said.

Griffin nodded. "Yes, I would. I'd like to discuss it with Merrie. To be honest, I think I would like to discuss it with her right now." He dropped the scraper in the bucket, then rubbed his palms on his thighs. "I'll be back in a few hours."

Early grinned. "You just take all the time you want, you hear? A lady shouldn't be rushed."

Griffin blinked in confusion, then nodded. "Thanks, Early. I appreciate your understanding."

With that, he turned and started for home. The trip back took only half the time that the trip to the harbor had, since Griffin was jogging most of the way. When he reached the cottage, he threw open the door and strode inside.

"Merrie?" The sound of his voice echoed throughout the house. "Merrie, where are you?"

"Merrie!" Ben squawked. "Merrie-girl!"

She emerged from the bathroom, a towel in her hand, her short hair damp and her rosy face looking as fresh and pretty as a dew-soaked flower. "What are you shouting about? Why aren't you at work?"

He crossed the room and grabbed her by the hand, then drew her toward the couch. "I have come to apologize," he said.

She watched him warily. A slow smile curled the corners of her mouth and she sighed. "Griffin, you don't owe me an apology. I'm the one who should apologize, for keeping all this from you. I just didn't know how to tell you, and I knew you would blame me."

"And I did," he said. "For that, I am truly sorry." He grabbed her other hand and wove his fingers through hers.

"I never meant for this to happen, Griffin, and I swear if I could change it, I would."

"I know."

"But I am not going to say I'm disappointed," she continued. "I refuse to say that. I'm happy you're here, especially if it will save your life."

"And I am happy to be here, too."

"You are?" Her eyes were wide with surprise.

"Yes. And I believe it is time to face the reality of this situation. I don't think I'm going to be able to get back, Merrie."

She bit her bottom lip and nodded. "I know."

"And if I was brought here to save my life, then I'd best get on with living it," he continued. "And to that end, I have made plans for us. Early Jackson has offered me a business opportunity. I will be able to provide a living for you. We can stay here on the island and make a good life for ourselves."

"You've decided this?"

"Yes. Of course, I am interested in hearing your opinion in this matter, but I know this is the right course to take."

She nodded. "I see."

"And I will say again that I believe we should get married. It seems the only logical step. We cannot continue to live together outside of wedlock. It would not be proper. Now, you may have your say in the matter, if you like . . . but it will not change my mind."

Merrie stared at him, openmouthed, her gaze clouded with disbelief. In that very instant, he knew he had said something wrong again. He just wasn't sure what the hell it was.

She jumped to her feet, then with a frustrated growl, she threw the damp towel in his face. "Go to work, Griffin. Because if you stay in this house one more minute, I swear, I will personally drop-kick you back to 1718 myself!"

With that, she turned and stormed into her bedroom, slamming the door behind her so loudly the house shook. Griffin stared after her, then sank back against the cushions and covered his eyes with his hands.

Maybe it would take more than one conversation with Early Jackson for Griffin to understand a twentieth-century woman.

AT FIRST, she couldn't sleep. All that had passed between them in the daylight hours now seemed to conspire to rob her of rest. Meredith tossed and turned, punching at the pillow and cursing Griffin's overbearing soul. She wanted to forget the man and his chauvinistic ideas! But even after she finally drifted off, thoughts of him still haunted her mind.

He came to her in a hazy dream, a dream she'd had so many times in the past, a dream that had left her without fulfillment, without release. But this time, it was different, for he was no longer a vague image that would evaporate upon waking, but a flesh-and-blood man, her fantasy come alive.

She felt the bed sink beneath his weight, the heat of his body near hers, and heard the sound of his soft even breathing. He gently placed his hand over her mouth and Meredith's eyes met the intense blue gaze above her as the pale moonlight streamed though the window to gleam on his tanned face.

"Do not speak, Merrie," he warned, his words soft and seductive and warm on her cheek. "For I'm still not certain that I should be here. One false word might steer me from my purpose this night."

He watched her for a long moment, indecision carved on his handsome features, then withdrew his hand. Slowly, she reached up and traced the lines of worry on his forehead with her fingertips, as if the simple gesture might erase any doubt he still had.

All their arguments suddenly faded and all their differences disappeared. In that instant, she knew that she loved this man, this proud and arrogant pirate, this man who held honor so dear. And she could no longer fight her feelings for him.

It didn't matter why he'd been brought here, whether she was saving his life, or he was saving hers. All she knew was that they belonged together, now and forever, in this bed and in this time.

Silently, she let her fingers drift along the planes and angles of his perfect face, exploring his striking cheekbones, his strong jaw, his sculpted lips, as if she were touching him for the first time. Weaving her fingers through his long hair, she drew his mouth down to hers.

A groan rumbled in the back of his throat as his lips covered hers, and he abandoned himself to their kiss. There would be no going back now, she thought. She had waited for Griffin her entire life. They would love each other in the deepest way possible, the consequences be damned.

His tongue gently probed her mouth and she opened to his ever-deepening kiss, the taste of him like a drug to her senses, numbing and addictive, and devastating in its power over her. This was like no kiss they had shared before, so filled with the promise of the passion yet to come.

She waited for a flood of trepidation to overwhelm her, for all her fears and insecurities to push to the surface as they had the other times. But she felt so right in his arms, like a sensual, self-aware woman, not a nervous, fumbling neophyte.

He pulled her beneath him and settled himself along the length of her body, his weight trapping her against his body, the evidence of his desire pressed against her belly, outlined by the tight denim.

Griffin pushed up and braced his hands on either side of her head, a self-deprecating grin twisting his lips. "It has been a long while since I've been with a woman."

She felt her face flame. "Almost three hundred years," she murmured, running her hand down the front of his T-shirt to the waistband of his jeans. "That is a very long time."

Through his T-shirt, she felt the hard muscles and the warm flesh of his torso. Suddenly, she wanted to rid him of all his clothes. She tugged at the hem of the shirt, pulling it up until it bunched beneath his arms, then ran her nails down along his spine.

He drew a sharp breath and held it, then groaned in pleasure. "I am not certain of how things go between a man and a woman in this century, so we will proceed . . ." He brushed a kiss across her lips. "Slowly."

"Slowly," Meredith repeated, her confidence bolstered.

"Slowly," he repeated, nuzzling her ear.

He rolled off of her, then sat back on his heels, his gaze never leaving hers. With a grin, he pulled his T-shirt over his head and threw it to the floor. In the moonlight, he looked as if he'd been carved from solid marble. She reached out and allowed her hand to drift along the tight muscles of his abdomen.

He took her hand and drew her up in front of him, then pulled her body against his, kissing her long and hard, cupping her backside in his hands, molding her hips to his.

Suddenly, desperately, she wanted to feel her skin warm against his. What wickedness possessed her, she didn't know, but she pushed against his chest, then grabbed the bottom of her nightshirt. In one easy movement, she yanked it up over her head, unashamed of what she revealed.

But while her arms were still stretched above her, Griffin's mouth drifted to her breasts. "So beautiful," he murmured, teasing at her nipple with his lips.

Meredith shivered, then tossed the nightshirt over her shoulder. "When you first met me, you thought I was a boy."

He glanced up at her and shot her a seductive grin. "I was suffering from a blow to the head. I am very clear of mind at present."

"Then make love to me, Griffin," she murmured, her fingers twisted in his long hair. "I want to show you that I'm a woman, your woman."

With that, they began a slow and easy love play, teasing and touching, whispering soft words of encouragement as they explored each other's bodies. Before long, her panties and his jeans ended up on the floor next to the bed, and they were twisted together, naked, with nothing standing between them.

She'd never felt such immense desire before, such overwhelming need. Every touch seemed so perfect, so filled with emotion. This was what passion was supposed to be like between a man and a woman. Not the awkward fumbling and frantic groping and nervous apprehension that she'd experienced in the past, but a tantalizing give-and-take, a hunger that seemed to grow by each second until she knew there had to be something more.

She needed to feel him not just around her and above her, but inside her. Hesitantly, she reached for him, touching him as she'd never touched a man before. He was like smooth silk and warm steel. With fleeting fingers, she ran her hand along the length of his shaft. He moaned softly and murmured her name. Then, as if to return the pleasure she gave him, he touched her in a way so intimate, she instinctively drew away.

"Don't be frightened of me, Merrie," he said. "Let me take you to a perfect place."

She relaxed and closed her eyes, surrendering to his gentle caress. Slowly, a delicious warmth seeped though her limbs, pricking at the tips of her fingers and toes. But gradually, the warmth turned to need. Her breath quickened and her every thought focused on the touch of his hand on her body. The tension built deep in her core until she moved against him, aching with need.

"Please," she whispered. "Please, Griffin. I want you."

Then his warm fingers were gone. In an instant, he was above her, the touch of his hand now replaced by his probing shaft. He drew her knees up along his hips and slowly entered her.

She winced as he met the proof of her virginity and she bit her lip, ready to face his surprise, his confusion, maybe even his disdain.

He frowned. "This cannot be so," he murmured.

"You are my first, Griffin," Merrie said, averting her gaze, a soft blush coloring her cheeks. "I've waited for you my whole life."

The confusion in his eyes gradually turned to understanding, then longing. He moved above her. "It may hurt, Merrie," he murmured. "But I vow, it will be the first and last time our lovemaking causes you pain."

She nodded. "I need you, Griffin."

He held her face in his hands and gazed deeply into her eyes. "And I need you, Merrie, my love." He moved against her and with one smooth thrust, took her.

For a long moment, he didn't move again, allowing her to adjust to the feel of him buried deep inside her. But then, as if he knew when the time was right, he pressed into her, slowly at first, then with a powerful rhythm.

Her senses reeled with every thrust and release, a pulse of tension quickening at her core. She whispered his name, again and again, a silent plea to bring her release. Higher and higher they climbed, rocking against each other until she felt as if she'd lost all touch with reality.

Suddenly, she was there . . . and in an instant, gone, tumbling over the edge, crying out at the same moment he did, their hearts and their souls merging into one. And in that glorious, shattering moment, she knew she belonged entirely to this man, this Griffin Rourke.

She always had.

8

MEREDITH SIGHED in contentment, fighting the pull of wakefulness and sinking back into the hazy world of sleep. The fantasy had become real, and oh so perfect. Her pirate had come to her in the middle of the night, taking her with unbridled passion and fierce possession. And she had given herself to him, body and soul, heart and mind, until, in an exquisite instant, they'd become one.

Nestling into the warmth of his embrace, she pressed her forehead against the silky black hair on his chest, then drew a deep breath through her nose. The smell of their lovemaking still lingered on his skin. She listened to the strong, even sound of his breathing for a long time, then slowly opened her eyes.

She smiled and sighed softly. It hadn't been a dream. Griffin was here, in her bed, his naked body lying beside hers, his long legs twisted around hers. And for the first time in her life, she felt complete, as if she had found her place as a woman. She had waited all her life for this man, knowing he was out there, somewhere. And across time and distance, against all odds, they had found each other.

She drew her foot up along his leg and let her sleepy gaze drift up his chest to his face. Softened by sleep, his perfect features looked boyishly vulnerable, not at all like the intense and powerful man who had made love to her. Would she ever truly know him? Or would he always keep a part of himself, that part that belonged to the past, from her?

Taking care not to disturb his sleep, Meredith slipped out of his careless embrace. She pushed herself up on her knees and studied him intently. Slowly, she pulled the sheet away from his waist, uncovering him to her eyes, determined to know his body as he seemed to know hers. He was flawless, and so beautiful. Reaching out, she ran her fingers down his chest, tracing the dark path of hair from his collarbone to his waist and below. Emboldened, she touched him there, softly stroking the essence of his manhood.

"Mmm. Would that I could wake up to that touch every day, Merrie-girl."

Snatching her hand away, she looked up in surprise to find him watching her through hooded eyes. "I—I didn't mean to wake you," she said, feeling a blush creep up her cheeks.

He reached out and took her hand, then kissed her palm. "Do not be frightened to touch me, Merrie. I want to feel your hands on me."

She had never felt such a deep and abiding trust in a man before. With Griffin, she sensed that anything she did would please him, from an innocent kiss to a carnal caress. This was the man she loved, the man she would spend her life with, and from him, she could hold nothing back.

With trembling fingers, she reached down and took him in her touch. He sucked in a sharp breath and closed his eyes, growing hard beneath her hand. As she stroked him, her confidence grew and she became acutely aware of the power she held over him. By just a simple caress, she could stir the embers of his passion until they flamed bright again.

"God, Merrie, what you do to me," he murmured, his eyes closed, his expression tense with tightly held longing.

Slowly, she lowered her head and kissed him, the heat of his erection branding her lips. He moaned and twisted his fingers through her hair, holding her still for a moment above his finely muscled stomach.

She knew of the things that could be between a man and woman, yet never thought she would want to try them herself. But now, it all seemed so natural. She wanted to love him in this way, too, to experience every facet of intimacy with him.

Gently, she ran her tongue along the ridge of his desire, then took him in her mouth. As she moved over him, she listened to the sounds he made deep in his throat, taking her cues from his reactions. And then, as her movements quickened, his breathing followed suit, and she knew he was close.

In one smooth movement, he pushed himself up and grabbed her around the waist, whispering her name in a soft, urgent voice. Drawing her body above his, he spread her knees to straddle his thighs. His hands pushed down on her hips until she impaled herself on him, slowly, exquisitely, sinking onto him until she felt the whole of him deep inside her.

"Oh, my," she cried, breathless.

"Be still." His words were more a warning than a command. He held her there, keeping her from even the slightest movement. She shifted, trying to escape his iron hold. "Don't, Merrie," he breathed. When she stopped, he pressed his hand between them and gently touched her where they were so intimately joined.

Their gazes locked and she began to rock against him, drawing closer and closer to her peak. She felt herself slipping over the edge of the precipice and twisted above him, aching for more of his touch, allowing him a deeper thrust, knowing her release was near. And then, in the instant before it came, she felt her body tighten around him. She watched a myriad of reactions cross his face, pain, pleasure, surprise, but he refused to close his eyes and break their wordless connection.

He spoke her name once, and then again, the syllables borne on a desperate moan. She saw him tense, ready for his release and then, she let go, falling and falling, then swept aloft on a gentle draft of air, taking him with her in a soaring flight of sensual deliverance.

When they had both floated back to reality, he wrapped his arms around her and buried his face between her breasts, his breath still coming in hard gasps. She smoothed his hair with her fingers and smiled, content to stay as she was, joined with his body, touching his soul.

"No woman has ever done that to me," he murmured, his words hot against her skin. He drew back and looked up at her, a sheepish grin twisting the corners of his mouth. "'Twas . . . astonishing," he said. "Truly extraordinary."

"I'm glad I was your first," she replied, drawing her finger down his damp chest.

He took her face in his hands and kissed her, long and hard. "And I am glad I was your first, Merrie."

She grinned and turned her blushing face to the side. "I used to think I was silly for waiting as long as I did," Meredith admitted. "But now I know, I was waiting for you. Somehow, I knew you would come for me. First in my dreams, and now in real life. I think we were always meant for each other, Griffin."

"That is hard to dispute after the beauty we have shared together, love," he said.

Her heart skipped at his simple endearment. They hadn't said the words yet, but she knew how she felt. She loved this man, more than she ever thought it was possible to love. And whether he could tell her the same or not, it didn't matter, for she knew deep in his heart, he loved her, too.

"Are you hungry?" she asked.

"I could use a soda pop," he murmured, nipping at her shoulder. "And some of that cold pizza."

"For breakfast?" Meredith laughed. "It hasn't taken you long to develop a taste for twentieth-century food, has it? I'll make you something more nourishing. We have to keep up your strength."

She slipped naked from the bed, breaking their carnal connection with a soft sigh. She felt his eyes follow her as she moved about the room, picking up his clothes scattered over the floor. Yet, she made no move to cover herself, for she felt no embarrassment at his silent appreciation.

"It's chilly out here," Meredith said, rubbing her arms.

"Then come back to bed," Griffin said. "I'll find a way to warm you."

She picked up a pillow as she passed the bed and tossed it at his head. "I'm hungry. Why don't you close your eyes and go back to sleep. I'll make some breakfast and we'll eat in bed."

He held the pillow over his face and spoke in a muffled voice. "I vow I'll need all the rest I can get in order to keep that sweet smile upon your face, Merrie-girl."

Merrie walked across the bedroom and opened the closet door. As she reached for her robe, her foot struck a cardboard box at the back of the closet, and something fell on her toes. She bent over and picked it up, then froze, a familiar musty smell touching her nose.

A wave of anxiety overwhelmed her and she grabbed the door to steady herself. Suddenly, all the events of that fateful night came rushing back at her, the wind, the rain, the fear. Everything coalesced in her mind until all she could see was the book she held—the gold inlaid letters, the worn leather-bound cover, the strange warmth seeping into her fingers and the vibrations. *Rogues Across Time.* She repeated the words silently to herself, her lips forming the words. *Across time . . . across time.*

She glanced furtively at the bed, relieved to find Griffin's face still buried beneath the pillow. Then she snatched her robe from the closet and tugged it on, tucking the book into the pocket.

"Would—would you like coffee?" she asked, trying to keep her voice light and even.

He pulled the pillow from his face and grinned. "Mmm," he replied. "Coffee. And orange juice. And some of those toaster waffles with jam."

She forced a smile in return, then hurried out the door. When she reached the kitchen, Meredith finally let the breath she was holding escape her lungs. "No," she murmured, throwing the book into the tall wastebasket beside the refrigerator. "No, it can't be. Not now. Please, not now!"

She sat down at the kitchen table and pulled her feet up, never taking her eyes off the wastebasket. A shiver raced through her, and she wrapped her arms around her legs and hugged her knees close.

"I just won't tell him," she said. "He never has to know that I know." She felt a tear spring from the corner of her eye and she angrily wiped it away. "He's come so far for us to be together. He's happy here now. I can't give him up. Please don't make me give him up."

She sat alone in the kitchen for a long time, trying to rationalize her behavior, trying to convince herself that what she was about to do was right. But no matter how she tried, her conscience told her differently. In the end, she retrieved the book from the trash.

The decision was not hers to make, it was his. And if their love was meant to be, then it would be based in truth and trust between them. For she knew, if she kept this from him, it would return to destroy them someday. Besides, she couldn't be certain that he would choose to return. After all that had passed between them, maybe he would want to stay.

As if in a trance, she walked back to the bedroom, every step she took tearing at her resolve. She pushed open the door, then stood and watched him silently. He slept again, his arm thrown over his eyes, the sheet twisted around his waist. Her heart tightened painfully and she could barely breathe. But she moved into the room and sank onto the bed beside him.

With a sigh, he pulled his arm from his eyes and turned a sleepy gaze in her direction. "Is breakfast ready?"

She shook her head and held the book out in front of her, praying that he wouldn't take it.

"What is this?" He glanced up at her and frowned. He reached out and touched her cheek and stared at his damp fingers. "Merrie, you are crying! What is wrong?"

She nodded at the book. "That's it," she said, her voice shaking with emotion.

"What are you talking about?"

She bit down on her lower lip to keep it from trembling, then reached down and clumsily opened the book. He levered himself up in bed and she placed it in his lap. "There," she said, stabbing at it with her finger. "The picture of the pirate. That's how you came to be here."

He stared down at the illustration. "I don't understand. This is just a drawing."

"You see, I forgot all about this," she said, her voice sounding as if it belonged to someone else. She drew a ragged breath. "I was looking at this picture the night of the hurricane. I focused on it, trying to forget how frightened I was. And then the book turned warm and it seemed to hum with life. The wind stopped and I crawled out of the closet and I walked outside." She brushed a tear from her cheek with the back of her hand. "And—and then I found you on the beach."

He stared down at the book, then ran his palm across the yellowed page. "*This* is how I came to be here? This book?"

"I—I'm sorry, Griffin," Meredith said. "I forgot all about it. I was so scared during the storm and then you turned up and I never thought about it again. And—and then, it just dropped on my foot while I was getting my robe from the closet."

He stared down at the book for a moment, then looked up into her watery gaze. "Tell me what this means," he said softly.

"You know what it means," she said.

"I want you to say it, Merrie."

"I—I think it means you can go back . . . if you want."

"And what do you want?" he asked.

"Don't ask me that," Meredith said. "Don't ask me to make your choices for you, because I won't." A sob broke from her throat. "I won't!"

He pushed the book aside and pulled her into his arms, stroking her hair as she wept. "Don't cry, Merrie. Please, don't cry. Everything will be all right, I promise."

But his words were little consolation, for in her heart, she knew he would leave. And when he did, nothing would ever be right in her world again.

THEY SPENT the rest of the day in bed, making love, sleeping, and then making love again. Griffin brought her to completion with his fingers and his mouth and his body, each time trying to drive every thought of his departure from her mind. But no matter how he pleasured her, he couldn't erase the sadness from the depths of her gaze.

Though they had avoided all discussion of his decision, it still stood between them, looming like a storm on the horizon. She knew he needed to leave, and so did he. Yet by not speaking of it, they could still deny what midnight would bring. And with each hour that passed, the clouds came closer and Merrie's anxiety grew.

Finally, as the time for his leaving neared, he pressed his lips against her temple and inhaled the sweet scent of her hair. "Tell me that you understand," he murmured.

He glanced down at her, but she refused to meet his gaze. She seemed a million miles away. He wanted to draw her back, bring her close, so they might spend their last hour together as they had the past twenty-four. But he knew it was time to talk.

"I don't," she said. "I don't understand."

"I have left part of myself back there," Griffin explained. "Something unfinished. A debt to my father, and my family name. And until I finish with Teach, I can't live here. I won't be . . . whole."

"He's not responsible for your father's death," Merrie said.

He nodded. "I know that now. You helped me to see that. But I still have a job to finish. He has to be stopped and if I'm not there to see it done, it may not happen. Who knows how many more people he will harm before he meets his end?"

She sniffled. "I should have left the book in the trash. I should have never told you."

He placed his finger beneath her chin and turned her green gaze up to his. Tears swam in her eyes, but she valiantly fought them back. "But you did," he said, "and it was the right thing to do."

"I don't want you to leave."

"Merrie, I wouldn't leave unless I was certain I'd be able to return."

She pushed herself up and braced her arms beside him, looking down into his eyes. "You can't know for sure whether you'll be able to come back. We're not even sure how you got here—beyond the book. And that may not even be it."

He slipped his hand over her nape and drew her closer, covering his mouth with hers. He drew deeply of the heady taste of her, knowing it would have to last him a very long time . . . perhaps forever. "What we share transcends all time and space, Merrie-girl. I refuse to believe that we will not be together. If not in this lifetime, then in another."

"What am going to do without you?"

He pulled her down onto this chest and held her head to his heart. "You're a strong woman, Merrie. Stronger than any woman I have ever known."

"I don't feel very strong right now," she said in a small voice.

They stayed that way for a long time, her arms wrapped around his waist, her cheek pressed against his chest. And then, as if they both knew it was time, she loosened her grip and pushed away from him, turning her tear-stained face from his gaze.

Griffin pushed back the sheets and sat up on the edge of the bed, raking his hands through his hair. He felt her touch on his back and reached over his shoulder to clasp her hand. "I swear to you, it will be all right."

He waited until her fingers loosened, then drew his hand away and stood.

"Your clothes and boots are in the hall closet." Her voice was even, dispassionate, as if she'd already distanced herself, to stave off the pain.

Slowly, he walked from the room, then gathered his clothes and dressed. He found the leather purse, on the mantel where it had lain untouched for nearly a month. When he was dressed, he returned to the bedroom.

She was sitting on the bed, wrapped in her robe, looking much smaller and frailer that she had just minutes ago. "Is it time?" she asked, refusing to glance at the clock for herself.

"Not yet," he said.

"I can't do this," Merrie said, her head bent. "Please don't make me."

"You can do this and you will. For me. Do you remember what to do?"

"Tell me again," she said.

"Do exactly what you did that night, the night I came here."

"And then what? If it works, how do I get you back?"

"You have told me that Blackbeard will meet his end on November twenty-second. At midnight on that day, you must summon me, the same way you did during the storm."

"And what if you don't come back?"

"You summoned me here once and you can do it again. I will come back."

"Unless you're dead," Merrie said, her voice cold. She turned to him, a suddenly desperate look in her eyes. Her fingers clutched at his waistcoat. "Promise me you won't die. I promise not to grieve if you don't come back, as long as you don't let yourself get killed."

He knelt down in front of her and pressed her hands between his. "Merrie, 'tis time. You must gather your courage and do this one last thing for me now."

She took a long look at him. "I'm going to close my eyes," she said. "And when I open them, I want you to be gone. No goodbyes." Her eyelids fluttered shut, but a tear escaped and traced a path down her smooth cheek. "I'll pretend it was all a wonderful dream."

Griffin stood over her for a long time, looking down at her lovely upturned face. Then he gently brushed his lips across hers, tasting the salt from the tears she'd cried.

"I refuse to hope that this works," she murmured, her eyes still closed.

He smiled. His beautiful Merrie-girl, stubborn to the very end. He took one last look at her face, then turned and walked out of the bedroom, leaving his heart and his soul behind.

The beach was bathed in a silver light from the nearly full moon. A gentle breeze rustled the leaves of the live oaks and the boughs of the tall cedar. He drew a deep breath, the tang of salt thick in the night air, then slowly walked to the water's edge.

The urge to rush back inside the house and pull her into his arms was strong. He turned around and stared at the light filtering from the bedroom window, trying to imagine Merrie inside.

She would crawl out of bed and pick up the book from the bedside table. He held his breath as he saw her figure pass in front of the light.

Then, she would turn off the light and step inside the closet. He watched the window go black.

"It's all right, Merrie," he murmured. "You can do this. I know you can."

He waited, counting down the seconds until midnight. Suddenly, the air around him went deathly still. The night sounds stopped—no crickets singing, no trees rustling, even the waves were silent.

He looked up at the sky, but it was no longer black. The stars had faded into a shimmering blue background, alive with swirling cyclones of light. The wind picked up and the ground shifted, throwing him forward. His legs were swept out from under him and he felt himself falling.

He looked down to see nothing beneath his feet except a great gaping darkness. Fighting back a flood of panic, he closed his eyes and threw out his arms, bracing himself for an impact, preparing to die.

And then, the moment before the ground rushed up to meet him, once more he felt the urge to turn back, to take shelter in Merrie's arms and to stay in her time. Regret surged through him and he cried out her name. Then everything around him went black.

A BRISK AUTUMN BREEZE sent a shower of orange and yellow maple leaves floating through the air and drifting down around Meredith's feet. The breeze was unusually warm for mid-November, following so closely on a series of chilly nights that had set the trees aflame with color in tidewater Virginia.

Meredith sat on a weathered wooden bench and stared out across Crim Dell, a lovely little spot in the center of campus. Across the pond she watched as young couples strolled over the picturesque footbridge. Several couples stopped atop the graceful arch and kissed. She frowned as she tried to recall the legend that was told about the bridge.

"They say if a young woman walks over the Dell bridge alone, she is doomed to spinsterhood. I wish someone would have told me that before I started jogging over it three times a week."

Meredith smiled and stood at the sound of Kelsey's voice. "Hi, Kels." She reached over the bench and gave her best friend a hug.

Dressed in a rumpled blazer and a skirt, Kelsey circled the bench and sat down beside her. "Imagine my surprise when I got your message this morning." She handed Meredith a paper cup. "Cappuccino with almond flavoring. Your favorite."

Meredith pulled the top off the cup and peeked inside. "Decaf?" she asked.

Kelsey laughed. "Since when have you given up the benefits of a high-caffeine diet?"

"I'm trying to cut back," Meredith said.

Kelsey shrugged and took the cup back. "What are you doing back here? I figured you were blissfully happy on that island of yours. After all, I haven't heard from you since our hasty little visit in September. So, did you do it? I've been dying to know!"

"Don't tell me you've spent the last two months speculating on the state of my sex life."

Kelsey nodded. "I think about it when I'm not contemplating Bernoulli's derivation of Boyle's Law. Particle physics and sex have many commonalities, you know. So, did it happen?"

Meredith felt the tears pushing at the corners of her eyes. "Yes, I—we—" Her voice caught in her throat. "I'm sorry."

Kelsey stared at her with a concerned gaze. "What's wrong, Meredith? You might as well tell me now, because you know I'll get it out of you sooner or later. Was it that bad?"

Meredith stifled a sigh. Whenever Dr. Kelsey Porterfield happened upon a puzzle, she didn't give up until she had figured it out. And though Meredith had managed to shuffle her out of the cottage without an explanation, she knew she'd have to come up with one now.

"It was wonderful," Meredith said. "Everything I'd imagined it would be."

"So, what's wrong?"

"He's gone," Meredith said.

Kelsey's hopeful expression fell. "Oh, no. I'm so sorry." She slipped her arm around Meredith's shoulder.

"He left over a month ago. And—and I think I'm pregnant." Though she'd suspected as much for the past week, she confirmed the fact with a home pregnancy test and a visit to her doctor earlier that morning. Yet, this was the first time she'd admitted it out loud. Suddenly, it was no longer just a concept, but a reality.

"Oh, my," Kelsey breathed, her eyes wide with surprise. "What are you going to do?"

Meredith forced a shaky smile and placed her hand on her stomach. "I'm going to have a baby," she replied.

She wasn't sure when she'd first suspected she was pregnant. One day she'd been convinced that her problems were merely a result of the stress of Griffin's departure, and the next day, she just knew. Somehow, she had sensed the life growing inside her and from that moment on, she'd loved the child with all her heart and soul.

These sudden and intense feelings, the instinct to protect her baby, filled her with wonder. She'd never believed she would have children. Now, she would have Griffin's child and she knew, in her heart, that this was right.

"Can you do this alone?" Kelsey asked.

"Yes, I can. But I'm not sure yet that I'll have to."

"Does he know about the baby?"

Meredith shook her head. "No. Not yet."

"Where is—" Kelsey cursed softly. "Can we at least call him by name here? He's not some deity, at least not in my book."

"His name is Griffin," Meredith said softly, letting the sound of his name linger on her tongue. "Griffin Rourke."

"Where is this Griffin Rourke?"

"He's gone," Meredith replied. "He had to go . . . back home . . . to take care of some business."

"What kind of business?" Kelsey demanded, a note of disdain in her voice.

"Family business," Meredith said.

"So is he coming back?"

Meredith bit her bottom lip and tried to stem a flood of emotion. "I don't know. But I'll find out tomorrow night at midnight."

"What happens at midnight?"

"At midnight tomorrow night, November twenty-second will be over. I'm supposed to . . . call him . . . to see how he is."

"Then you know where he is?" Kelsey asked.

Meredith sighed. How she wished she could tell Kelsey everything. At least her friend might be able to give her some hope or encouragement. But Kelsey would never believe everything that had happened in the past two months. "Not exactly."

"But you have his phone number. You said you were going to call him."

"But he might not be there," Meredith said. "In fact, that's why I came back. If things don't work out, I'm moving back here right away. I talked to Dr. Moore today and told him I wanted to teach that seminar in colonial American history for next semester."

"So rather than face your problems head-on, you're going to retreat into your work. If I were you, I'd go after the bum. And if you don't, I will."

"I—I can't. And neither can you."

Kelsey shook her head in disbelief. "Just where did this Griffin go that you can't find him?"

Meredith laughed softly. "You wouldn't believe me if I told you."

"Try me," Kelsey challenged. "I've heard them all, from 'The dog ate my homework' to 'I was abducted by aliens the night before my final exam.' Whatever you say, I'll promise to believe you."

Meredith drew a deep breath. Maybe if Kelsey knew the truth, she might be able to help. After all, she was a scientist. She had to have an open mind about the unknown. "Remember when I asked you about traveling in time?"

"Yes," Kelsey replied.

"Well . . . that's it." The words rushed out of her along with a tightly held breath.

Kelsey scowled. "What's it?"

"Time travel."

"What about time travel?" Kelsey asked.

Meredith sighed inwardly. How was she supposed to explain without sounding like a lunatic? Kelsey could be very protective when her friends were troubled. The last thing Meredith needed right now was Kelsey fussing and hovering over her. "You see, I . . . well, he . . . I'm not going to write a novel," she said, the last sentence tumbling out of her mouth unbidden. "After all, everyone knows that time travel just isn't possible."

"Of course it's not possible. At least not now," Kelsey confirmed. "But I told you that in September."

"And I listened," Meredith replied, swiftly altering her course, knowing that now was not the time to tell Kelsey. "I've decided to finish my Blackbeard book. And I'm going to take on a few more classes next semester, so when I have the baby I can afford to take some time off."

"Are you sure you're ready to raise a child alone? It's hard enough with two people."

"I love Griffin," Meredith said. "And I know he loves me. And even if we can't be together, I'll have a part of him with me because I'll have his child."

"Did he *tell* you that he loves you?"

Meredith shook her head. "I know he does. He's just not very good at expressing his feelings. He loves me, Kelsey."

"Then why did he leave?" Kelsey demanded.

Meredith closed her eyes and tipped her head back, letting the breeze blow against her flushed face. "He had no choice." She opened her eyes and gave Kelsey a sideways glance. "Can you at least be a little bit happy for me? What happened between Griffin and me was wonderful. And even if I never see him again, I'll never, ever regret it."

"How can I be happy when your life is in chaos? I'm worried about you, Meredith. You've always kept such tight control over your emotions. You've led such an orderly life. Now you're a wreck. Look at you. You look like you haven't eaten in days."

Meredith pushed to her feet and hoisted her bag up on her shoulder. "I haven't. So why don't you buy me lunch at that pretty little tearoom on Prince George Street. Then, I've got a long drive back to Ocracoke. I borrowed a car from Tank Muldoon and he needs it back by morning."

"Why don't you forget about going back?" Kelsey asked. "Stay here."

"I can't. All my research is still at the cottage. And I've paid the rent through the end of December. But if you're so worried, you can come down and pick me up before Christmas."

"I should have never agreed to take you down there in the first place. I feel like this is partially my fault. I should have talked you into staying in Williamsburg to work on that damn pirate book."

Meredith looped her arm in Kelsey's and grinned. "You know I never listen to you, Kels."

"I know," Kelsey said with a pout.

"But you're still my very best friend in the world. You always will be." Meredith tugged on Kelsey's arm and they started off in the direction of College Yard. As they walked through the Sunken Garden, Meredith looked at every beautiful building, every ancient tree and every perfect flower. This was her home and she felt safe here. If Griffin didn't come back, she would find a way to be happy here again.

Strange how quickly life changed. For the longest time, she couldn't imagine being content anyplace but William and Mary. Her career had been her whole life. Though she had worried over publication and tenure and class assignments and campus politics, she'd reveled in her life and her research.

The whole time, she'd never realized there was something—or someone—missing from her life. And now, in such a very short time, Griffin had carved out a place for himself in her heart and soul, a place she never knew existed. She could imagine being happy anywhere, as long as she was with him. And if not with him, then with their child.

When they reached the center of College Yard, Meredith stopped and turned to take a long look at the Wren

Building. It stood sentinel over the campus, a picture of symmetrical elegance made of soft red brick. Its multipaned windows sparkled in the sun and the weathervane perched on the cupola clock tower swung with the vagaries of the autumn breeze. "It's very old, isn't it," she murmured, shading her eyes. "Hard to believe it's lasted three hundred years."

"I've never seen anyone so attached to a bunch of creaky old buildings as you are," Kelsey teased.

"I wonder how they looked when they were brand-new," Meredith said.

Griffin would know. She scolded herself inwardly. How many times did she think of him everyday? *I wonder what Griffin would think of this, I wonder what Griffin would say about that?* If he didn't come back, she would have to learn to put him out of her mind. She would focus all her attention on their child. And more important, she would choose to believe he was still alive and happy—somewhere.

But until she tried to summon him tomorrow night, she had to believe that he would return—to her and to their child.

9

OUTSIDE the gray-shingled cottage, an unrelenting wind whipped through the branches of the live oaks, sending up an eerie moan. Waves, roiling and ominously black, crashed against the narrow beach. In the sky above, the moon shone as it had the night he'd gone, the bright white light dimmed every few minutes by invisible clouds scudding across the night sky.

Meredith let the lace curtain drop from her stiff fingers and glanced at the clock next to the bed. Her heart skipped a beat. Eleven fifty-five. It was almost time. She closed her eyes and said a silent prayer, clutching the book to her chest.

"Please, please, let this work," she whispered, a desperate edge to her voice. "Send him back to me, safe and sound."

He wasn't dead. She'd spent the last month proving that to herself, searching every original source she could find— letters, journals, books—for any mention of his name. The day she found the name of the seaman mistaken for a pirate, she cried, for it wasn't Griffin Rourke.

Every night, from the night that he'd left, she'd stood on the beach and waited, hoping that by some miracle she would find him there. Some evenings, she would let the tears fall unchecked, allowing herself to fall prey to her emotions. On other nights, she would refuse to give in, knowing in her heart that they would be together soon. Sometimes, she'd even talk to him, as if he were right beside her, telling him all about the baby and the wonderful future they'd have together.

With trembling fingers, she lit the lantern. Ben Gunn was already in his place in the closet, squawking in protest. She'd even put on the same clothes she'd worn the night Griffin arrived, just for luck. Meredith searched her mind for anything she'd missed. For all she knew, she might have only one chance to bring him back and she wanted to make that chance count.

All the lights in the house were out, the phone was unplugged. She reached over and flipped off the bedside lamp, then opened the closet door. "Come back to me, Griffin," she said as she stepped inside. "Come back to me now."

Meredith sat down on the closet floor, pulling her knees up to her chest to wriggle into the cramped space. Slowly, she ruffled through the pages of the book until she found the picture of the pirate. Drawing a deep breath, she focused her gaze on the delicate ink lines that made up his handsome face, a face that looked so much like Griffin's.

"Awk. Shiver me timbers!" Ben screeched. "Thar she blows!"

"Come back," Meredith murmured, running her finger lovingly across the page.

"Aye, matey." Ben flapped his wings, his shadow wavering on the closet wall.

"Come back."

"I takes my man Friday with me!"

"Come back to me, Griffin. Now. Please."

"Come back," Ben mimicked.

Meredith stared at the picture for a long time, repeating her plea over and over again like a mantra. She wasn't sure how much time had passed, but suddenly she was acutely aware that the wind had stopped blowing. Holding her breath, she listened and waited. Then, with a cry of relief, Meredith stumbled to her feet and shoved open the closet door. Ben followed her with a flap of his wings.

"Griffin?" Her shout echoed through the dark, silent house. "Griffin!"

She ran through the rooms, the book still clutched in her arms, checking each shadowy corner before she headed outside. Though the wind had stopped, the waves still roared against the shore. For an instant, the moon appeared from behind a cloud and Meredith thought she saw a flash of white on the beach.

"Griffin!" She ran toward the water's edge as the moon slipped behind a cloud again. But when she reached the spot, there was nothing there. Turning frantically, she looked for any sign of him, but the beach was deserted.

"Griffin!" Her voice died against the roar of the waves. "Oh, God, Griffin, please. You have to be alive. Please, don't leave me here alone." A sob tore from her throat and Meredith dropped to her knees.

She opened the book and searched for the picture. A flood of moonlight spilled over the lawn, illuminating the page of the book. "You can't be dead," she cried. "I'd know it. I'd *feel* it." She drew a ragged breath and watched as a tear dropped onto the yellowed page. "I love you, Griffin. I will always love you, wherever you are. I will always—"

A sharp crack of thunder obliterated her words. Meredith looked up, startled by the sound. A violent shiver rocked her body and she cried out at the sight before her.

The sky had turned an eerie, luminescent blue and the water below looked like liquid silver, glowing with its own light. Transfixed, Meredith watched as the ghostly images of three square-rigged ships appeared before her eyes, then faded again, behind a shroud of vapor.

Thunder split the silence again and Meredith jumped, her breath catching in her throat. The acrid smell of gunpowder filled the air and she realized that it was not thunder she'd heard, but cannon fire. She tried to crawl to her feet, but her legs refused to move. A cacophony of sound descended around her—men shouting, pistols firing and the unnerving boom of cannons.

From out of nowhere, the wind began to blow, swirling and screeching around her until her eyes watered and her ears rang. The book blew from her hand but she managed to grab it before it had blown too far. Meredith curled into a ball and covered her head with her arms, screaming in terror against the chaos.

And then the ground lurched beneath her and the noise grew more intense, more distinct. Panic was upon her, so overwhelming she felt as if she might be sick. And then the wind stopped as suddenly as it had begun.

Hesitantly, she lifted her head and risked a look around, squinting against a bright light. She still held the book clutched against her chest, but it was no longer night, it was day. And she was no longer in her backyard, but inside a small rowboat. Her gaze followed the length of a tall mast above her and her heart stopped as she came upon a familiar flag snapping in the breeze.

A horned skeleton, white on a black background, held an hourglass in one hand and a dagger in the other. "In league with the devil," Meredith whispered numbly, "and your time is running out." And beneath the dagger, a red heart and three drops of blood. "Surrender," she continued, "or blood will be drawn."

Shoving the book under a mildewed canvas at the bow, she got up and peered over the edge of the rowboat, only to find herself on board a larger ship. Blackbeard's ship!

And from what she could tell, she was caught in the midst of a battle.

All around her, a ragtag army of pirates swarmed the deck, gathering near the cannons that lined one side of the sloop. Many of the men held small wooden kegs under their arms and others hurriedly lugged cannonballs from one side of the ship to the other.

"We've cut the villains in half!"

Meredith turned toward the booming voice. A towering hulk of a man stood in the center of the deck, a man she'd only seen in her mind's eye and old illustrations. But now, the pirate Blackbeard stood before her. And he was alive!

Edward Teach cut a fierce figure, tall and broad-shouldered, his waist-long beard twisted into strands, his bushy black mustache covering his mouth. Over a ragged coat, leather belts crisscrossed his chest with a brace of pistols looped in each. He wielded a cutlass in his left hand and a cocked pistol in his right.

"Damnation," Teach shouted. "The cannons have put us aground!"

Meredith watched, concealed in the ship's tender as the battle of Ocracoke Inlet began to unfold before her eyes. The events were happening exactly as she knew they would. As the crew scurried to refloat the ship, Lieutenant Maynard's two sloops were reeling from the pirate's eight-gun broadside attack. Half of Maynard's Royal Navy contingent was already dead or wounded.

Frantically, Meredith scanned the deck for Griffin. Was he on board the pirate ship? Or had he sailed with Maynard's crew? All she knew was that she had to find him, for she had been dropped into this place and time for a reason. And in her heart, she believed it was to save his life.

Slowly, she pushed to her feet. But before she could get a good look around, the ship lurched again and she tumbled headfirst out of the tender and into a musty pile of wool blankets. The deck rolled beneath her. The *Adventure* had broken free of the sandbar.

With her head down, Meredith crawled to the rail and wedged herself into a secluded spot behind a coil of rope. Blackbeard's ship lay just off the southern tip of Ocracoke. And out in the Sound, on the other side of the sandbar, Maynard's two sloops were struggling to free themselves from a shallow shoal. The *Ranger* looked badly damaged, but Maynard's other sloop was now afloat and closing the distance between it and the *Adventure*.

Meredith squinted across the water at the oncoming sloop. She could clearly see the men on deck, could even hear their shouts. Had there been no danger to her own safety, she could have called Griffin's name, but she remained silent, watching, waiting, fearing discovery.

And then her gaze fell on a familiar figure, standing at the rail of Maynard's sloop. She rubbed her eyes and looked again, then offered up a silent prayer of gratitude. He was still alive! Thank God, Griffin was still alive!

The breeze whipped his long dark hair around his face and fluttered the full sleeves of his white linen shirt. He, too, gazed across the water, his eyes fixed on the bow of Teach's ship. Did he know she was here? He couldn't possibly see her, but could he sense her presence?

With growing trepidation, Meredith watched as history happened before her eyes. Most of the men on board Maynard's ship had mysteriously disappeared, leaving only a few to be seen. Meredith knew they were waiting below deck, on the lieutenant's order, for Blackbeard's men to board. Only then, would they spring from the hold and attack. After what seemed like hours, the *Adventure* bumped alongside the deserted sloop.

"They were all knocked on the head but three or four," Blackbeard shouted in glee. "Blast you—board her and cut them to pieces!"

Emboldened by the order and armed with pistols and crude hand grenades, the pirates threw the grappling irons out across the bulwarks of Maynard's ship. Before they jumped the rail, they tossed the lit grenades onto the deck. After the explosions, Blackbeard boarded first, followed by ten of his pirates, all of them howling and firing their pistols at the slightest movement.

Through the thick smoke from the hand grenades, Meredith saw Maynard's crew emerge from below deck and engage the pirates in mortal combat. For an instant, she thought she saw Griffin again, but then he disappeared in the melee. Pistols flashed and cutlasses rang, and all around, men shouted.

The battle raged on, every man fighting furiously for his life, the wounded screaming in agony, and the dying shuddering with their last breaths. And in the middle of it all, Blackbeard swung his cutlass in a vicious slashing pattern, felling men all around him.

Again, she caught sight of Griffin, but then lost him. To board the sloop and find him would be folly. Without a weapon, she'd be dead before she took two steps. But she couldn't just watch as the man she loved fought for his life.

And then, she knew it was nearly over, for she had read the account of Blackbeard's final offensive over and over again. First, Lieutenant Maynard engaged the pirate. They both pulled pistols and took aim. Blackbeard's shot missed, but Maynard's tore through the pirate's body. Still, Teach fought on, the powerful blow of his cutlass snapping Maynard's sword at the hilt. The lieutenant fell backward, struggling to cock a second pistol. With perverse delight, Teach held his cutlass aloft, ready to deal Maynard a death blow.

"Rourke!" Maynard shouted.

A tall figure stepped out of the smoke, pistol drawn, sword at the ready.

With a howl of rage, Blackbeard turned on Griffin, the spy who had betrayed him. He swung his cutlass wildly and Griffin jumped back, throwing up his sword in defense, blocking the vicious blow. But the wounded pirate was crazed with fury, attacking like a man gone mad. As Griffin feinted and blocked each thrust of the cutlass, Maynard struggled to his feet to aid his friend and join in the fight. Crazed and bleeding, Blackbeard fought off the lieutenant's advances, as well.

Meredith scrambled out from her hiding place and made her way along the rail of the empty pirate ship. "Griffin!" she shouted.

For an instant, he turned away from the battle and met Meredith's gaze, his expression frozen in disbelief. "Merrie?" That was all it took for the pirate to take an advantage. He raised his cutlass over Griffin's head.

"No!" Meredith screamed. Griffin spun around, then ducked, fumbling for his pistol. He aimed blindly, firing at point-blank range. Blackbeard stumbled backward from the force of the ball, his cutlass dropping to his side, his hand clutching at his neck.

Griffin didn't look back. He fixed his gaze on Merrie and with relentless determination, he fought through the surge of pirates to reach the rail. Meredith waited, crying out with each blow he deflected. Suddenly, he was so close she could nearly touch him. She called his name as he leaped on board the *Adventure*, but as she reached out for him, she saw a pirate aim a pistol at Griffin's back. With a cry of alarm, she threw herself against Griffin's body and shoved him aside.

A searing pain shot through her arm. She stumbled, clutching Griffin's arm, then looked down to find blood slowly soaking her sleeve. She smiled. The pain didn't really matter. All she felt was overwhelming relief, for she knew that it was her blood and not his.

Slowly, her knees buckled and everything around her dissolved into darkness.

WITH A VIVID CURSE, Griffin grabbed Merrie and quickly shielded her from the battle raging behind them. "God's teeth, Merrie, what the hell are you doing here?" he shouted over the noise. "And how did you end up on Teach's ship?" She didn't reply and he cursed again. But as he tried to steer her toward the far rail of the *Adventure*, she seemed to be fighting him, like a dead weight in his arms.

"Merrie?"

He looked down in confusion, only to find her limp and boneless, her eyes closed, her face pale and blood seeping through her right sleeve.

He closed his eyes and fought a flood of emotion. "Oh, Lord, no," he whispered. In one swift movement, he scooped her up into his arms and carried her out of harm's way.

Griffin's mind raced, fear for Merrie's life burning in his throat. He had to get her away from all this chaos, before the tide of the battle turned again. Though Blackbeard had fallen, his men still fought on. And one of them had shot Merrie.

The *Adventure* was deserted except for a few cowering retainers, servants who worked on board but did not choose to fight. He spotted the ship's surgeon peering out from behind a barrel.

"Come here!" he ordered. "She has been wounded. You must help her!"

The old man shook his head, his rheumy eyes defiant.

"You cannot just let her bleed," Griffin cried. "By God, you are a surgeon, man. Do your job!"

"Not fer a traitor, nor fer a traitor's woman. Let her bleed, fer I will not lift a hand to aid her."

Griffin drew his pistol and took careful aim at the man's head, but the pirate surgeon merely laughed.

So be it. If Merrie was to live, then *he* would be the one to make it so.

Griffin glanced over his shoulder to see a pair of Teach's men retreating onto the deck of the *Adventure*. Considering the surgeon's hostile opinion of him, an armed pirate might pose an even greater danger to both himself and Merrie. He had to get her off this ship!

Griffin strode along the far rail. Lashed to the stern of the boat was a small tender the pirates used to ferry themselves to shore after dropping anchor. With single-minded purpose, he set Merrie down on the deck, drew his dagger from his boot and sliced through both ropes. He pushed the boat off the stern and it dropped into the water with a muffled splash.

"I will take you from this hellhole, Merrie, and make you safe again, that I vow."

Keeping one eye on Merrie, he snatched whatever supplies he could put his hands on—three moth-eaten blankets, a small sail, a burlap sack filled with fresh vegetables—and tossed them all into the boat. Two kegs of fresh water and a pair of oars went over the rail next, bobbing to the surface to float beside the small boat.

Satisfied there was nothing more to salvage, he gently hoisted Merrie's unconscious body onto his shoulder and stepped over the rail. Their combined weight and the height from which he jumped plunged them both deep beneath the water. Kicking strongly, he pushed for the surface, then broke through.

Treading water, Griffin quickly checked Merrie's breathing, then swam toward the boat. After settling Merrie in the bottom of the boat, he went after the water kegs and the oars. In less than a minute, he was rowing toward the southern tip of Ocracoke Island, to safety.

"You should not have come," he muttered, as if she could hear him. "I told you to wait and summon me when this was all over." She didn't respond, and he fought back another surge of fear. He'd been in the midst of the battle, yet had emerged without a scratch, only to see her, innocent and unaware, wounded by a pirate's pistol.

From the moment he'd left her in her own time, he'd regretted his decision. Damn his stubbornness. He didn't need to confront Teach to feel like a whole man! He felt that way when he was with Merrie. Every night since he'd landed back in his own time, he'd stood on the waterfront gazing out at the horizon, waiting for her to call him back, hoping she might not hold fast to their agreed-upon plan. She had, and now, she was in mortal peril. And it was all his fault.

He rowed hard, until he was drenched in sweat and his muscles burned in protest. Finally, after what seemed like an eternity, he felt the sand beneath the boat. Scrambling over the side, he pulled it up on shore. In the distance, he could still hear sporadic pistol shots, but the battle seemed to be drawing to a close. He had no way of knowing who had triumphed, but he had to trust Merrie's history books.

The pirates would be captured and he and Merrie would be safe on Ocracoke until help arrived.

Gently, he gathered her in his arms and carried her onto the beach, then settled her at the base of a dune. Dropping to his knees, he held her close, cradled against his body. She was so cold and still. "Do not leave me, Merrie," he whispered against her cheek. "I traveled across time to find ye, and I will not lose ye now."

Bracing her against his chest, he tore the sleeve of her blouse away and examined her wound. The ball had grazed the fleshy part of her upper arm and the bleeding had already slowed. "'Tis not as bad as I thought," Griffin murmured, needing to hear his own words as comfort.

He hastily retrieved the sail and spread it out on the sand, then laid Merrie on top of it. With his dagger, he pried the plug from the water keg. The pungent smell of rum wafted up to his nose. "Damn," he muttered. He took a long swallow to calm his nerves. "We will use it to clean your wound, Merrie-girl, for 'tis not fit for you to drink." He snatched up the other keg and prayed that it would contain water. If Merrie grew feverish, he'd need fresh water and finding it on Ocracoke was near to impossible.

To his relief, the keg did contain water, stale but potable. He gently washed her wound and then poured a bit of rum on it for good measure. His linen shirt, torn into strips, made adequate bandages, and before long, he'd made her as comfortable as possible.

The afternoon sun was warm and the breeze gentle, so Griffin laid the wet blankets over a stand of sea grass, knowing they would be needed as soon as the sun began to sink below the western horizon. "Tomorrow morning, there will be fishermen and trading ships passing near this island," he said, pressing her against his bare chest for warmth. "But for tonight, we are on our own, Merrie."

Griffin lay down on the sail and pulled Merrie against his body, taking care not to jostle her wound. He pressed his lips to her forehead, relieved to find that she hadn't grown feverish. Her skin felt cool and smooth and he gave her a soft kiss. "Wake up, Merrie-girl. Wake up and look at me with those emerald eyes of yours. Come on, Merrie." He reached down and stroked her temple with his fingers, watching her face, drinking in the sight of her after so many days apart.

Her eyelids fluttered, then opened. She looked at him with a groggy gaze. "Griffin?"

He smiled. "Hello, Merrie-girl."

"You're alive," she murmured. "I've missed you so much."

"And I have missed you," he said. "More than you will ever know. How do you feel?"

She frowned. "I—I hurt. My arm. What happened?"

"Nothing for you to worry about. You will be fine. I swear I will let no harm come to you."

She gazed up at him sleepily. "Good. I'm fine...the baby...is fine. We're all...fine." Her eyes slowly drifted shut. Griffin pressed his palm to her forehead. She did feel a bit warmer. He cursed softly. The fever was starting and she was losing touch with reality. She was mixing up his past with her present, his dead child with her injury.

He grabbed what was left of his shirt and soaked it with water, then dabbed it on her forehead. "I will not lose you, Merrie. We will have a long life together, you and I."

While Merrie slept, Griffin built a fire at the base of the dune, big enough to provide some warmth, but small enough not to attract attention. There was no way of knowing whether any of the pirates had escaped the battle, and he was ill prepared to deal with them now.

As he bent over to throw another piece of driftwood onto the fire, Merrie cried out his name. She sat straight up, her glazed eyes frantically searching for him, her breath coming in short pants.

"I—I thought you were gone."

He returned to her side, gathering her into his embrace. "I am here. I will not leave you, I promise."

Her breathing gradually calmed and he felt her relax in his arms. "I'll never leave you," he said, tracing the perfect curve of her bottom lip with his thumb. "You taught me to love again. After I lost Jane, I was dead. All I cared about was finding a way to numb the pain, first with drink, then with women and then with my scheme to bring down Teach. You were right, though. He didn't cause my father's death. And I think I knew that all the time.

"But I felt empty for such a long time, and my thirst for vengeance seemed to make me feel again. Even though it was hate, at least I felt alive. And then I met you, and you saved my life, first on your beach and then on the *Adventure*, but most important, you saved me with your love.

"And slowly, all the hate seemed to drain out of me and I was filled with you. I should never have left you, Merrie." Griffin smiled and shook his head. "I loved you and I let you down. And someday, maybe I will be able to say this all to you again, so you might hear me and understand. But for now, know that I love you more than life itself."

Griffin touched his mouth to hers then buried his face in her silken hair. How could he have been such a fool? If he'd stayed with her as she'd begged him to, she would never have been hurt. But in his stubborn quest for vengeance, he had risked her life, and for that, he would never forgive himself.

During the night, Merrie's condition worsened. She tossed and turned, crying out in pain. She fought against the blankets, but as soon as he removed them, she began to shiver violently. He drizzled rum and water into her mouth with the rag and spoke softly to her of the life they would share and the love in his heart. She babbled of pirates and babies, begged for Kelsey and screamed at someone named Delia. And then she talked to her mother and father as if she were still a child.

Finally, she drifted off to sleep, the rum finally taking effect. Sleeplessly, Griffin watched her, listening to her ragged breathing, counting the minutes until dawn and cursing his inability to help her.

And sometime, during the darkest moments of night, he began to pray, begging God to spare the only woman he had ever loved. A woman who held his heart and soul in her very hands.

THE WORDS CAME to her in a haze. *Go to sleep, Merrie-girl. And if I am gone when you wake, you will think this has all been a dream.* A dream . . . a delicious dream.

Meredith slowly opened her eyes, squinting against the bright light. For a moment, she wondered where she was, but then she nestled beneath the blanket and sighed. She'd just sleep a bit longer. Maybe if she was lucky, she could slip back into the fantasy again. The pirate . . . the battle . . . the bedroom. This time, it seemed so real.

But as she tried to go back to sleep, the rest of the world seemed determined to wake her up. A cool breeze chilled her face and the gulls and the waves were particularly loud this morning, adding to the nagging headache she had. She reached up to pull the blanket over her head and a sharp pain shot through her right arm.

"Ouch!" she cried, then opened her eyes. "What the devil is—"

"You're awake. How do you feel?"

With a cry of surprise, Meredith shaded her gaze and stared up at a tall shadowy figure that blocked the light. The silhouette was familiar, broad shoulders, narrow waist, muscular legs...and long hair that whipped about in the breeze. Her dream . . . could this be her pirate? Meredith slowly raised herself, bracing against her good arm.

"Griffin?" she asked softly.

"I am here, love."

"You're Griffin."

He squatted beside her and smoothed her hair back from her eyes, staring at her in concern. "Of course I am, Merrie-girl. Who did you think I was?"

Meredith shook her head, trying to marshal her jumbled thoughts. Her pirate was here. This wasn't a dream. He was real and his name was Griffin. Suddenly, it all came flooding back to her. She glanced around, not recognizing her surroundings. She was on a deserted beach. Her eyes fixed on a small boat pulled up on the sand and she frowned. She'd seen that boat before . . . but where?

"Where are we?"

"On Ocracoke. My Ocracoke, not yours."

"Wh-what happened?" she murmured.

"You were wounded during the battle. You've had a fever, but you're all right now."

"I traveled back in time," Meredith said. "I was waiting for you on the beach and when you didn't come, I thought I'd lost you forever. Then, suddenly, the sky turned a strange color and I could see ships in Teach's Hole. And the next thing I knew, I was on the *Adventure*."

He kissed her softly. "When I saw you, I could not believe my eyes. Faith, but I was angry with you, Merrie. For disobeying me, for putting your life in danger."

"I didn't disobey you," Meredith said stubbornly. "I was on the beach at midnight, waiting, just as we'd agreed. Not that I don't have every right to disobey if I choose. You can be so domineering, sometimes."

Griffin tipped his head back and laughed. "I believe I have my Merrie back, sharp tongue and all. And perhaps I should be glad of it. Perhaps, without you there, I might have been torn asunder by a pirate's cutlass. Perhaps you have once again saved my life, Merrie."

"I had to," Meredith murmured. "I couldn't lose you." She tugged him down next to her and laid her head in his lap, losing herself in his nearness. "I never want to lose you again, Griffin."

"I am well aware that I do not express my feelings eloquently," Griffin said softly. "But 'tis *I* that could not bear the prospect of losing you."

She snuggled against him, wrapping her arms around his waist. "I'm here now, and I'm not going anywhere."

He bent down and kissed the end of her nose. "But I nearly did lose you. You were feverish for so long and I could do nothing for you. And there was no help to be found. I had nearly decided to row you across the Sound, when you seemed to rest easier."

Meredith frowned, a sudden uneasiness assailing her senses. "How long was I sick?"

"Two days."

Instinctively, her hand fell to her stomach. "The baby? Is the baby all right?"

Griffin's gaze filled with worry. "Merrie, you were delirious. There is no baby."

"Of course there's a baby," she said. "*Our* baby."

He patted her hand sympathetically. "Close your eyes and get some rest. You are still feeling the ill effects of the fever."

She reached up and gently touched his cheek. "Did I forget to tell you about the baby?" She shook her head. "I can't tell the difference between what's real and what was part of the dream. I was sure I told you. We *are* going to have a baby, Griffin."

He stared at her, his expression emotionless save for a muscle twitching in his jaw. "A baby? You are certain of this?"

"I went to the doctor yesterday. Well, not exactly yesterday..." She paused and smiled, trying to hide her confusion at his cool reaction to her news. She was sure he would have been happy. "More like tomorrow, two hundred seventy-eight years in the future. You—you don't look pleased," she stated glumly.

He sighed and got to his feet, then began to pace in the sand beside her. "To be honest, Merrie, I am not. 'Tis not what I would have chosen for you."

"If you're worried about my reputation, don't be."

He laughed harshly. "I am not worried about your reputation. That can be solved easily enough by marriage."

"Why do all your proposals sound like direct orders? What if I don't want to marry you?"

He glared at her, his eyebrow arched. "You *will* marry me, of that you can be certain."

"I will decide if I will marry you or not."

He continued to stare at her, waiting, a sardonic smile on his face.

"I can't imagine a more pitiful proposal," she muttered.

Griffin groaned and raked his fingers through his hair. "I do not mean to be dictatorial . . . or boorish." He knelt in the sand beside her and clasped her left hand between his. "Meredith Abbott, I love you, damn it. Will you do me the great honor of becoming my wife?"

A smile curled the corners of her mouth and she giggled. "You're forgiven, Griffin Rourke. And yes, I think I will become your wife."

His stern expression cracked and he chuckled, then kissed her palm. "I want to spend my life with you, Merrie."

"And the baby?" she asked. "Do you want our baby?"

He ran his fingers through his hair. "Of course I do. It's just that, I—I want to grow old, with you beside me."

"We can do that," Meredith cried. "Women have had babies for years, Griffin. I'm healthy and our child will be healthy." She paused and studied his tense profile for a moment. "But this isn't about me, is it? This is about Jane."

His head snapped around and he stared at her. "I could not have saved her, even if I had been there. Merrie, you mean more to me than anyone I have ever known. I could not stand to lose you. It would kill me."

She placed her palm on his cheek. "I'm not Jane and won't die, Griffin. Not until we've spent at least the next fifty years together in this world, and eternity together in the next."

He looked out at the water, refusing to meet her eyes. "Things are different in this time, Merrie," he said, frustration edging his voice. "You know what the medical care is like here. I cannot help thinking that you would have been better off staying in your own time. At least I would have known that you, and the child, were safe."

"But we don't have to live here," she said. Her statement came right out of the blue, but she knew she spoke the truth. She blinked hard, then gazed over at the boat on the beach. Suddenly, it all came back to her. That where she'd seen the boat, on Blackbeard's ship. And in side the boat was the book. Meredith laughed out loud, her uncontrolled giggles causing a frown of concern on Griffin's face.

Griffin placed his palm on her forehead to check for fever. "I don't know where the book is, Merrie. I wish I did, for I would not force you to stay here against your will. Would that I could take us both back to your time."

Meredith drew a deep breath and stilled her laughter. "The book is in the boat," she said, pointing to the beach. "It's in the bow, beneath an old canvas."

He looked at her in disbelief. "How do you know this?"

"Because *I* put it there," she said.

Griffin stared at her for a while as if trying to judge her lucidity. Then he stood and jogged down the beach to the boat. When he returned, a smile curled the corners of his mouth. "We can go back," he said, his voice filled with relief. Suddenly, with a shout, he bent over and grabbed Meredith around the waist and pulled her up against him, lifting her feet off the ground. Just as quickly, he placed her in front of him and cupped her face in his hands, raining kisses over her face.

"We can go back," he repeated. "You'll be safe, the baby will be safe and we will live a long and happy life together."

She looked deeply into his pale eyes. "Is that what you want? To live in my time?"

"Yes," Griffin said. "I should have never left."

"You don't want to stay here?"

He growled at her. "On this, I know my mind. I love you, Merrie-girl, more than life itself. And I have come to realize this in so many ways since we have been apart. If living in your time will mean more time together, for us and our child, then that is where I want to be."

Meredith hugged the book to her chest and gazed at the man who had traveled across time to find her. He was right. They were meant to be together and nothing would ever separate them again. She raised herself on her toes and wrapped her arms around his neck.

"Then I think it's time for us to go home, Griffin Rourke. We have a long adventure ahead of us and I want it to begin right now."

Epilogue

MEREDITH SAT in the middle of the living room floor in the gray-shingled cottage on Ocracoke Island. A brisk autumn breeze blew in through the screened porch, teasing at her hair. Piles of books surrounded her as she packed the stacks in large cardboard boxes. Beside her, two-year-old Thomas Griffin Rourke, named after his paternal grandfather, played with a large ball and babbled to himself.

"Is there a reason we bring all these books to the island every summer?"

Meredith turned around to see her husband standing in the doorway that overlooked the Sound. He looked much the same as he had that first night, only now he was dressed in twentieth-century clothes. "Yes, there is," she said with a wide smile. "It's so you can carry them back and forth to the car and I can admire your incredible physique."

Griffin chuckled and knelt beside her. He placed his hand on her swollen abdomen. "The last time you admired my incredible body, sweetheart, we made another baby."

"But it was fun, wasn't it?" She covered his fingers with hers.

Griffin nibbled at her neck playfully. "Yes, 'twas fun, Merrie-girl. But I would have been well satisfied with just one child. I would not have risked you again."

Meredith wrapped her arms around her husband's neck and kissed him on the mouth. "When are you going to realize that having your children is the most precious gift I can give you?" she asked, pressing her forehead against his.

"And 'tis the most precious gift I can give you, as well," he murmured.

They both turned to gaze at their son. He now stood beside the boxes, methodically pulling out books and tossing them onto the floor with unabashed glee.

"If your son doesn't stop, we'll never get out of here," Griffin said.

Meredith leaned over and grabbed Thomas around the waist, then pulled him, giggling, into her lap. She kissed his cheek and he screeched in delight. "Why don't you take *your* son outside," she said. "I've just got these two boxes to pack up. One goes with us and the other goes to the island library. Trina's going to pick out the books she wants and donate the rest to charity."

Griffin grabbed his son and hoisted him up on his shoulders. "Take your time, sweetheart. We'll be down on the beach."

Meredith watched as the two most important people in her life walked through the door and headed out to the water. "Time," she murmured, distractedly repacking the boxes. "Once I thought we'd never have enough time together. But now, we have all the time in the world, don't we, my love."

She smiled winsomely and picked up an old volume from the floor. As she stared at it, she ran her fingers across the worn leather-bound cover and over the gold inlaid letters.

"Rogues Across Time," Meredith read. Wistfully she recalled the first time she had picked up the book. If the hurricane hadn't driven her into the closet that night so long ago, she may never have found her pirate. The book had changed her life.

She moved to put the book in her keeper box, then at the last moment, she gently placed it inside the other box—the box meant for the library. "Maybe someone else will be lucky enough to find their soul mate somewhere in time," she said softly. "And maybe someday, they'll find the happiness that I have."

Satisfied with her decision, Meredith taped up both boxes and called her husband and son back in from the beach. No, she didn't need the book anymore. All her fantasies had become reality and she was living her dreams every day of her life.

BRIDE'S BAY RESORT

UNLOCK THE DOOR TO GREAT ROMANCE AT BRIDE'S BAY RESORT

Join Harlequin's new across-the-lines series, set in an exclusive hotel on an island off the coast of South Carolina.

Seven of your favorite authors will bring you exciting stories about fascinating heroes and heroines discovering love at Bride's Bay Resort.

Look for these fabulous stories coming to a store near you beginning in January 1996.

Harlequin American Romance #613 in January
Matchmaking Baby by Cathy Gillen Thacker

Harlequin Presents #1794 in February
Indiscretions by Robyn Donald

Harlequin Intrigue #362 in March
Love and Lies by Dawn Stewardson

Harlequin Romance #3404 in April
Make Believe Engagement by Day Leclaire

Harlequin Temptation #588 in May
Stranger in the Night by Roseanne Williams

Harlequin Superromance #695 in June
Married to a Stranger by Connie Bennett

Harlequin Historicals #324 in July
Dulcie's Gift by Ruth Langan

Visit Bride's Bay Resort each month wherever Harlequin books are sold.

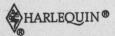

HARLEQUIN®

BBAYG

MILLION DOLLAR SWEEPSTAKES
AND
EXTRA BONUS PRIZE DRAWING

No purchase necessary. To enter the sweepstakes, follow the directions published and complete and mail your Official Entry Form. If your Official Entry Form is missing, or you wish to obtain an additional one (limit: one Official Entry Form per request, one request per outer mailing envelope) send a separate, stamped, self-addressed #10 envelope (4 1/8" X 9 1/2") via first-class mail to: Million Dollar Sweepstakes and Extra Bonus Prize Drawing Entry Form, P.O. Box 1867, Buffalo, NY 14269-1867. Request must be received no later than January 15, 1998. For eligibility into the sweepstakes, entries must be received no later than March 31,1998. No liability is assumed for printing errors, lost, late, non-delivered or misdirected entries. Odds of winning are determined by the number of eligible entries distributed and received.

Sweepstakes open to residents of the U.S. (except Puerto Rico), Canada and Europe who are 18 years of age or older. All applicable laws and regulations apply. Sweepstakes offer void wherever prohibited by law. Values of all prizes are in U.S. currency. This sweepstakes is presented by Torstar Corp., its subsidiaries and affiliates, in conjunction with book, merchandise and/or product offerings. For a copy of the Official Rules governing this sweepstakes, send a self-addressed, stamped envelope (WA residents need not affix return postage) to: MILLION DOLLAR SWEEP-STAKES AND EXTRA BONUS PRIZE DRAWING Rules, P.O. Box 4470, Blair, NE 68009-4470, USA.

FAST CASH 4033 DRAW RULES
NO PURCHASE OR OBLIGATION NECESSARY

Fifty prizes of $50 each will be awarded in random drawings to be conducted no later than 6/28/96 from amongst all eligible responses to this prize offer received as of 5/14/96. To enter, follow directions, affix 1st-class postage and mail OR write Fast Cash 4033 on a 3" x 5" card along with your name and address and mail that card to: Harlequin's Fast Cash 4033 Draw, P.O. Box 1395, Buffalo, NY 14240-1395 OR P.O. Box 618, Fort Erie, Ontario L2A 5X3. (Limit: one entry per outer envelope; all entries must be sent via 1st-class mail.) Limit: one prize per household. Odds of winning are determined by the number of eligible responses received. Offer is open only to residents of the U.S. (except Puerto Rico) and Canada and is void wherever prohibited by law. All applicable laws and regulations apply. Any litigation within the province of Quebec respecting the conduct and awarding of a prize in this sweepstakes may be submitted to the Régie des alcools, des courses et des jeux. In order for a Canadian resident to win a prize, that person will be required to correctly answer a time-limited arithmetical skill-testing question to be administered by mail. Names of winners available after 7/30/96 by sending a self-addressed, stamped envelope to: Fast Cash 4033 Draw Winners, P.O. Box 4200, Blair, NE 68009-4200.

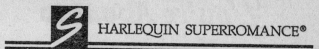

HARLEQUIN SUPERROMANCE®

From the bestselling author of
THE TAGGARTS OF TEXAS!
comes

Cupid, Colorado...

This is ranch country, cowboy country—a land of high mountains and swift, cold rivers, of deer, elk and bear. The land is important here—family and neighbors are, too. 'Course, you have the chance to really get to know your neighbors in Cupid. Take the Camerons, for instance. The first Cameron came to Cupid more than a hundred years ago, and Camerons have owned and worked the Straight Arrow Ranch—the largest spread in these parts—ever since.

For kids and kisses, tears and laughter, wild horses and wilder men—come to the Straight Arrow Ranch, near Cupid, Colorado. Come meet the Camerons.

THE CAMERONS OF COLORADO
by Ruth Jean Dale

Kids, Critters and Cupid (Superromance#678)
available in February 1996

The Cupid Conspiracy (Temptation #579)
available in March 1996

The Cupid Chronicles (Superromance #687)
available in April 1996

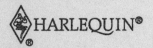